SAY IT WITH BULLETS

Two abused and neglected children find sanctuary with a neighboring rancher. Out West, a gold prospector's widow must evade the clutches of a corrupt sheriff. Defying doctor's orders, a wounded cop searches for his missing rebellious sister. After fleeing Hitler's Berlin, a Jewish father and daughter will find unexpected danger in California. A girl's dowdy stepmother is hiding a dangerous secret. And in the gritty underbelly of professional boxing lurks a bloody mystery whose reverberations will echo down several decades.

Books by Arlette Lees
in the Linford Mystery Library:

ANGEL DOLL
CODE OF SILENCE
MIDNIGHT RAIN
HOLLYWOOD HEAT
A FROZEN SILENCE
SILENCE OF THE BONES

ARLETTE LEES

SAY IT WITH BULLETS

Complete and Unabridged

LINFORD
Leicester

First published in Great Britain

First Linford Edition
published 2019

A catalogue record for this book is available from the British Library.

ISBN 978–1–4448–4048–3

Published by
F. A. Thorpe (Publishing)
Anstey, Leicestershire

Set by Words & Graphics Ltd.
Anstey, Leicestershire
Printed and bound in Great Britain by
T. J. International Ltd., Padstow, Cornwall

This book is printed on acid-free paper

Last Chance in Gunnar

I, and my eleven-year-old brother Duke Wayne, lit out of the trailer as soon as the ashtrays started flying. We hid in the pickup in the carport as neighbors gathered at the curb in gossipy knots. It's hard when you're a kid and people think you'll never amount to a hill of beans. It's not like we picked Heidi and Gaylord out of the social register. We got stuck with our parents just like they got stuck with us.

Deputy Wittler pulled up in his patrol car, the light bar flashing red and blue on the pocked skin of our single-wide. He'd been here so many times that we called him Jason like he was a member of the family. He ignored the sounds of fighting and breaking glass coming from inside the thin walls and walked straight to where we were hunkered down on the bench seat.

'What got 'em going this time, Bossy?' Jason asked.

Bossy, that's what they call me, because Evangeline is too big a name for a kid of nine. When I grow up I'm going to change it to something pretty like Cheyenne or Turquoise.

'Gaylord gave her money for groceries, and she bought a blonde wig and a bottle of gin,' I said. 'All we have in the kitchen is half a box of Lucky Charms and a pint of sour milk.'

Duke Wayne sat silent, all bottled up with his arms crossed over his chest, muscles knotted in his jaw. He didn't let off much steam but I think things bothered him real deep.

Heidi was our worst nightmare but Gaylord was no prize either. When Heidi isn't mad at us kids she'd ragging on Gaylord for having the seven-year itch all twelve years of their marriage. He says when he steps into his fly-button jeans and rolls that pack of Camels in the sleeve of his Budweiser t-shirt, the ladies around the watering holes of Gunnar can't keep their hands to themselves.

'Let me see your back, Bossy,' said Jason.

'Not again,' I moaned. 'We did that the last time.'

'It's either me or that old bat from CPS.'

I let him lift the back of my shirt so he could examine me for bruises.

'Those cigarette burns are from years ago,' I reminded him. 'Heidi said it was an accident and it would never happen again. I was too little to remember anything about it.'

'So, Social Services threw you back in the ring for one more round.'

'Something like that.'

The trailer door burst open and Gaylord tumbled into the dirt patch we called our front yard. He was bleeding from a cut above one eye. Heidi stood in the doorway, a cigarette dangling from her mouth. She wore silver spike heels with a tattered bathrobe and the chain of a silver fish-scale purse looped around her wrist. When I saw her like this, it was easy to forget how beautiful she was when she was sober and all dolled up.

She swung a gin bottle and let it fly, but instead of hitting Gaylord, it exploded against the door of the patrol car.

'Well, that's one she won't be drinking,' said Gaylord, scrambling over to the carport.

Heidi lost her footing and landed in a heap below the stoop. She looked toward us kids, her eyes wild and unfocused.

'Get in there and clean up that mess,' she slurred.

'You stay right where you are,' said Jason. He walked over and snapped the cuffs on Heidi's small wrists as a second patrol car arrived on the scene and Deputy Barnswallow got out.

'Take Mrs. Draper in and let her sleep it off,' said Jason.

'How about him?' said Barnswallow, nodding toward Gaylord.

'Not tonight. Get something out of the trailer she can be released in. Can't have her walking through town in her nightgown.'

The neighbors gawked when Barnswallow pulled away from the curb with Heidi banging her head against the window. When they were gone, Jason turned to my dad.

‘So, what’s your plan for these young ’uns, Mr. Draper?’

‘Well, we’re not going back in there,’ he laughed.

‘You’re not driving anywhere either,’ said Jason, catching a whiff of gin on Gaylord’s breath.

‘I’ll walk over to the Stardust, then.’

‘What about the kids? I won’t have them sleeping in the back of the pickup no more.’

‘They can work something out with the neighbors,’ he said.

Gaylord leaned into the truck window. He ruffled my hair and gave Duke Wayne a playful punch on the shoulder. ‘I’m not fit company right now,’ he said, with a lopsided grin. ‘I’ll hook back up with you and your mom tomorrow.’

I watched him walk into the October night toward the lights of Centennial Boulevard, the dead leaves swirling around his ankles until the night swallowed him whole.

I turned to Jason. ‘We have school tomorrow. My homework’s in there.’

‘I’ll get your stuff,’ he said ‘You got two

choices. Either I release you to a responsible adult, or it's going to be foster care again.'

Duke looked up. 'I want to go to Uncle Dan's.'

* * *

Dan was standing beneath the porch light when we pulled up in front of the ranch house. Duke walked inside with his baseball glove and bat, and I tagged along with our school books. Jason set our box of clothes and things inside the door.

'How long this time?' asked Dan.

'It's a drunk-and-disorderly. She should be out mid-morning,' said Jason.

'Fair enough.'

Dan Wellstone was a respected figure around Gunnar. He took pride in raising tough-as-nails cattle on the piss-poor homestead his family passed down to him. Heidi said Dan was a handsome sort if you liked the silver over-the-hill type. He had light green eyes and a handlebar mustache that he kept neatly trimmed and waxed. I'd never seen him in anything except his cowboy duds and a Stetson, but I knew he kept a good suit in the closet for funerals and jury duty. When Heidi and Gaylord went on a toot, he'd take us out to the ranch until things settled down.

That night the wind blew hard and cold off the reservation that backed on to the ranch. Sand and tumbleweed piled up against the back of the house. He fed us stew and biscuits from an iron pot on the stove and settled us in blankets by the fireplace like pick-of-the-litter pups.

The next day Duke and I got off the school bus in front of the trailer park. The pickup was gone and Mrs. Raley, the park manager, was sweeping broken glass out of the coach door into the dirt. Liquor fumes drifted all the way to the sidewalk.

'What's going on, Mrs. Raley?' I asked.

'What does it look like?' A metal curler slipped out from beneath the scarf tied in a bow at her forehead.

'Where are our parents?'

'I have no idea,' she said, with angry tears in her eyes. 'You people are out of here. You can tell that dad of yours that I'll see him in court. This coach is ruined.'

'We can help you clean things up,' said Duke.

She shook the broom at us and we backed away. 'It's people like you give trailer trash a bad name.'

'I'm a straight-A student, Mrs. Raley. I'm not trash,' I said.

'Give it a couple more years.'

'Come on,' said Duke, 'before the old witch climbs on her broom.'

We ran until we came to the truck stop outside the Silver Spur Café. After going from truck to truck looking for a ride, we hitched with a driver pulling a load of hogs to New Mexico. He showed us tattoos he'd got in seven states and said he was shooting for all the lower forty-eight. He pumped his brakes after a few miles and let us out in front of Uncle Dan's mailbox.

When we came to the top of the driveway, Dan was knocking dirt off a shovel against a fence post. He wiped the sweat off his forehead with a blue bandanna.

'Don't go behind the barn,' he said. 'I just killed a big rattler, and where there's one there could be more.' He leaned the shovel against the shed.

'We been kicked out of the trailer park,' said Duke. 'The truck's gone and nobody's there.'

'It's already three o'clock. Hasn't Heidi been by?' I said.

'Not yet. Why don't we call the jail and see what's holding things up? If she's still a handful they might keep her an extra day.'

We walked up the path to the house.

'One more thing,' said Dan, when we got inside. 'I don't want you kids hitching anymore. Even after you're back with Heidi and Gaylord, you need a ride, you call me and I'll come pick you up.'

Dan put in a call to the jail but they said Heidi had been released around noon.

'If the truck is gone, I imagine she hooked up with Gaylord,' said Duke.

'Even if they come and get us, we can't go back to the trailer.'

'I think we better make up the beds in the spare room,' said Dan, 'just in case they don't make it. Now, who wants to help me put the new water pump in the truck?'

Duke helped Dan, and I volunteered to

make up the beds. When Duke came inside we sat at the kitchen table and did our homework.

That night at dinner I ate so much chili and cornbread it was downright painful to breathe. By the time I finished drying the dishes it was dark and I knew that no one was coming for us. It was a relief to sleep through the night without Heidi dragging us out of bed to clean up the trailer or giving Duke Wayne a whipping because she was in a bad mood. Gaylord didn't hit us, but he didn't help us either. Dr. Moss said that Duke Wayne was the youngest ulcer patient she'd ever treated.

'Get your jackets,' said Dan, reaching for his hat. 'Let's drive into town and see if the new water pump does the trick. Maybe hook up with Gaylord and Heidi.'

The manager at the Stardust Motel said our dad had checked out at eight. That would have been hours before Heidi was released from custody. We cruised the bars along Centennial Boulevard — The Do Drop Inn; The Dead Man's Hand; The Cave. By the time we hit The Leprechaun Lounge we were plum out of ideas.

Uncle Dan looked up and down the strip and gave his mustache a thoughtful twist.

'I don't think we'll find them until they want to be found,' he said.

Duke became quiet. He looked at me, then at Dan, then back at me again.

'What?' I said. 'Have I grown two heads?'

'You two have the same shade of green eyes.

'I know,' I said, 'the same as Mrs. Raley's cat.'

'Don't that beat all,' said Uncle Dan. 'Bossy must take after her mom's side of the family, just like you take after Gaylord's side with your brown ones.'

We climbed back in the truck. 'How about a nice big piece of pie at the Silver Spur?' said Dan. 'You two could use a little meat on your bones.'

I was already full, but I managed to get it down.

* * *

A month later, a letter addressed to Heidi arrived from Gaylord. It had been forwarded from the trailer park to the ranch. He said he'd been working at the Lucky Friday Mine in Idaho's Silver Valley. A one-hundred-dollar bill was enclosed.

'That's weird,' said Duke. 'Heidi can't be with him if he thinks we're still in the trailer.'

Dan made an effort to track Gaylord down, but the mine closed when the price of silver dropped and the bookkeeper said he headed up Post Falls way with a Shoshone woman.

Dan smoothed out the one-hundred-dollar bill on the kitchen table.

'Can I smell it?' I said. Dan let me sniff it and Duke laughed at me.

'I just want to know how it smells to be rich,' I said, putting it back on the table.

'Well, it won't put you kids through college, but we can check out the big bookstore in Phoenix.'

The store was bigger than most of the dusty little towns I'd been in. I got a book on raising rabbits, and Duke got one on farm equipment repair. We took in a movie show and had dinner at Denny's before we started back to the ranch. We had a real fun time.

A week after our trip to Phoenix, Deputy Wittler pulled up in his patrol car, sending a big dust cloud over the corrals. Duke was tuning up the tractor engine in the shed and Dan and I were putting down hay for the horses.

'Morning, Deputy Wittler,' said Dan. 'Any word on Heidi?'

'That's what I was going to ask you.'

'Not a thing. We got a letter from Gaylord up Idaho way, but she wasn't with him. Last we heard, he was headed to Post Falls.'

'We gotta do something permanent about them kids, Dan. CPS gets involved one more time, a judge will probably make 'em permanent wards of the state.'

'Seems to me they're doing right fine where they are. I feed 'em right and their grades are up.'

'You the only relation they got?'

'Seems so.'

'Their uncle, right?'

'That's me.'

'And which side of the family would that be on, sir?'

'Heidi's side.'

The silence stretched out as Jason looked at the toe of his boot and kicked up a divot of dust. Finally, he said, 'That's good enough for me, Mr. Wellstone. Good enough for the time being, anyway. Have you considered filing a missing person's report on Heidi?'

'It's crossed my mind, sir.'

'Okay, let's give it another week or so. I'd hate to get stuck with a bunch of paperwork and find out she's just shacked up somewhere.'

* * *

That Christmas, Duke got a fully loaded toolbox and I got a breeding pair of Australian rabbits. We saddled up and rode out to Blue Canyon and ate chili around the campfire. It was the best Christmas we ever had.

The winter months passed slowly as winter always goes. One morning Duke and I rode the horses down to the road to pick up the mail. Duke's saddle creaked as he turned to look at me. As young as he was, I could see a bit of the adult in him.

'If they come back, I'm not going,' he said.

'Me neither,' I said. 'I'm never leaving the ranch.'

He looked at the grey sky. 'I'm going to get as far away from Gunnar as I can. I got some bad memories to switch out for some good ones.'

* * *

During the worst of the cold, the old cigarette scars started bothering me, and Uncle Dan took me to Dr. Moss, who prescribed a salve to apply at bedtime. Duke's old ulcer had healed, but he still slept poorly and had what was diagnosed as night terrors. I'd touch him gently on the shoulder to wake him and sit beside him until he fell back to sleep. It was one ailment the doctor didn't have the cure for.

It was a relief that Heidi had written us off, although from time to time I missed Gaylord and the way he used to ruffle my hair and tell us silly jokes. I just didn't want to live with him again. As the years passed, all I could recall was a wild-haired woman thrashing her head against a patrol car window, and a man who disappeared in a whirlwind of autumn leaves.

It was the summer between eleventh and twelfth grade when I drove the pickup into the yard and saw a woman with long black hair drinking from the garden hose. There was a bedroll and a backpack at her feet. I took her for an illegal immigrant seeking water and shade. I let her be and walked past her into the house.

A man sat at the kitchen table with Dan. He looked vaguely familiar.

'Say hello to your dad,' said Dan.

I was caught off-guard and couldn't think of one intelligent thing to say. He looked twice the age and half the size of the man I remembered. He had broken capillaries on his nose and a couple teeth missing up front.

'So, you're driving now,' he said.

'Have been for a while.'

'Dan tells me that Duke Wayne is a helicopter mechanic in Iraq. He always did want to see the world.'

'He's actually National Guard. He should be working stateside, but the military twists the rules when it suits them.'

'He's a strong kid. He's got the Draper blood going for him.'

I didn't consider that any great shakes, but didn't find it necessary to reply.

'Ever see Heidi after that night you went to the Stardust?' I asked.

'Never did. Guess she moved on. I do better with Winona. Age and a few ailments have slowed me down some. We're just passing through, and thought we'd stop and say hi. Her dad is in bad shape, so we're headed north to see him one more time before he goes.'

I wanted to say something meaningful, but too many years had passed between us.

'Well,' he said, scraping back his chair and stretching, 'looks like I've taken up most of your daylight.' He held out his hand and Dan shook it.

'Like I said before, you and Winona are more than welcome to bed down here for the night.'

'Thanks anyway, but we gotta find us a trucker going north.'

Gaylord turned to me and patted my shoulder. 'I'll write when we get settled somewhere.' I nodded. We both knew he wouldn't. It was just something you say to fill an awkward moment.

Without a word I wrapped my arms around his thin shoulders, the man in the cowboy boots and the fly-button jeans and the Camels tucked into his sleeve. I smelled the smoke in his hair, the whiskey on his breath, and out of nowhere I found myself holding back tears. He pulled back and held me at arm's length.

'You turned into a right pretty girl, Bossy.'

'Have a safe trip,' I said.

I watched from the window as he and the Shoshone woman gathered up their things and headed for the highway. A few years later I heard Gaylord died of a stroke somewhere in north Idaho.

Duke Wayne came home on furlough a

couple times. He looked older and war-weary, still haunted by nightmares and ghosts of his childhood. Nevertheless, he'd found his niche in the military, and he was good at what he did. On his third tour of duty, the boy who was named after a movie cowboy returned home in a flag-draped box. Dan took his good suit out of the closet for the funeral. He handled his loss with stoic grace like he handled everything else, but he was never quite the same after that.

The third day of the round-up was unseasonably hot.

'When you saddle Navajo, would you mind tossing a saddle on Buckwheat?' asked Dan. I felt the earth shift slightly on its axis. Dan had always insisted on saddling his own horse. I was told that even as a little kid he'd climb on a fence rail and drag the saddle onto his horse's back.

'Sure thing,' I said. 'Go finish your coffee.'

He patted me on the shoulder. 'All these years you've been my right hand, Bossy.'

That night, after a long day in the saddle, Dan went to bed and didn't wake up in the morning. He'd kept his cancer diagnosis secret for the past year.

* * *

A few days later, I sat across the table with our family lawyer, Amos Benchley.

'I'm going to skip all the legalese,' he said. 'The bank account, the Certificate of Deposit, the ranch and everything in it — all goes to his biological daughter.'

I was confused. 'Biological daughter?' I said. 'He never married. You'd think he'd have mentioned a child in all these years.'

'He never married because his daughter's mother was married to someone else.'

'I see.'

'He left everything to Evangeline Draper. That, my dear, is you. He's not Heidi's brother like he made out, and she's no Wellstone. She's a Haversham.'

'I've never heard that name before.'

'Well, it's a fact. Dan was an old friend of the family. He and Heidi linked up for a brief period of time when Gaylord was carrying on with that waitress from the Silver Spur. Heidi was really something to look at before the booze took over.'

'This is an awful lot to swallow in one bite, Mr. Benchley.'

'I think you'll manage. He left you pretty well-off by Gunnar standards.'

That evening, I cried as I went through the things I found in the attic trunk. I found photos of my great-great-grandmother, Evangeline Harper Wellstone, the lady who homesteaded this land. When I got around to changing my name, it wasn't to Cheyenne or Turquoise. I became Evangeline Wellstone, the person I was always meant to be.

* * *

The next spring found me digging in the garden patch behind the barn while the earth was still soft from the April rains. I turned over the tired soil one shovelful at a time, taking in the scent of warm earth, tossing aside buried bottles and rusty old cans.

About twenty inches down I unearthed the end of a slender chain caked with dirt. I tossed the shovel aside, bent over and gave it a gentle tug. There was a slight resistance before it surrendered to my hand. It was attached to a rotten piece of cloth covered with sequins that crumbled off in my hand. It was the sad remnant of a silver fish-scale purse.

I turned it over along with a million old memories. The burns. The belt. The booze. Foster parents who didn't want us kids except for the money, and one good man who gave us a forever home.

I leaned against the barn, breathless and weak in the knees. I remembered the day when Dan told us he'd killed a rattler behind the barn, but the significance of his words didn't resonate until now. I took a deep breath, grabbed the shovel and kept digging. This time the slender spike of a lady's high heel poked to the surface.

I tried feeling something — anything — for the woman who'd carried that purse and worn that shoe, who'd bought a blonde wig and a bottle of gin with the grocery money the day before she was killed. Maybe someday I'll evoke a tender thought or produce a single tear, but today is not that day.

I could have dug deeper, but I already knew what I'd find. Perhaps the earth has a right to the secrets it keeps. I dropped the purse and shoe back in the hole, covered it with soil and tamped it down with my boot.

I already knew everything I needed to know.

Bad Blood at Dry Rock

Deep in Vulture Canyon, an old prospector found my husband's remains beside his mule. Both had been shot once in the head, the saddle bags emptied, his six-shooter gone. The gun, with its bent barrel and loose chamber, was useless. It would probably have blown up in Ralph's face had he had time to unholster it.

Forgive me if I don't wear black veils and widow's weeds, but Rolf didn't know I existed once he began his love affair with gold. Because I was stranded in a leaky tent on the banks of Lost Horse Creek at the tail end of summer, I dutifully cried a few tears and got on with the business at hand.

Except for half an ounce of gold dust, a tired mule, a laying hen and a handful of clothes and cooking utensils, I was flat busted.

I'd never wanted to leave our homestead in the Midwest to strike it rich in the Wild West, but Rolf was a stubborn German, the kind who was always right.

Now, he was dead right.

I packed up Old Tom and headed for Dry Rock. It was just as dry and dusty as its name implied, but it was where we'd purchased supplies and made a few friends, and there was really nowhere else to go.

Like most wives who were dragged west, only to be widowed or abandoned, I was left with three options. I could starve, sell my virtue for two bucks a pop, or — well, I hadn't figured out option number three. All I knew was that I wasn't ready to go with choices one or two.

I had a few things working in my favor. I was young, pretty and determined to survive. If I was going to starve, I might as well have stayed in Ireland where I was born.

Once I arrived in Dry Rock I pitched my tent in the vacant lot between the Last Chance Saloon and Quan Lee's general store. Lee was a handsome young man who'd been born in San Francisco and spoke English well. Except for holidays when he wore red and gold embroidered silk, he wore traditional black from head to toe. His store carried a little of everything, but the bulk of his wealth came from outfitting gold miners.

Lee was the closest thing Dry Rock had to a doctor. At the back of his store he kept bottles and jars of mysterious powders, potions and elixirs labeled with Chinese characters. Occasionally, a white patient, under the cover of darkness, would leave with medication to cure his ills, often at night and through the back alley door.

'Good afternoon, Mrs. Kraus,' said Lee, as I lay my purchases on the counter.

With my long auburn hair and light green eyes, the name didn't seem to suit me any more than my late husband had.

'I think I'll go back to my maiden name, Susan Coyne, now that Ralph is gone.'

'Gone, Miss Coyne?'

'Gone, as in dead, Mr. Lee. Shot for gold that probably had less value than the bullet that killed him. He got more sand in his boots than gold in his pan.'

'My deepest condolences. Perhaps he was born under an inauspicious alignment of the planets.'

'I can't think of a better explanation, Mr. Lee.'

Lee measured out a small amount of gold dust and returned the remainder to its small satin pouch.

'I hope you don't mind my setting up camp in the lot until I figure out my next move.'

'A quiet neighbor would be nice for a change,' he said, gesturing toward the saloon. 'There's a rain barrel at the side of the store. Use what water you need.'

His eyes rested for a moment on my face, his expression enigmatic. I smiled, held his gaze for a moment, then looked away. Perhaps he was wondering how long a woman with limited resources could last in a place like this. I wouldn't mind having the answer to that myself.

That evening I watered Old Tom and placed Miss Penny in a box of straw in the tent. I bathed by lantern light, then lay awake listening to the rowdy uproar from the saloon, the sound of shattering glass, the drunken laughter of the bar girls, the scrape of boots as fights erupted on the boardwalk. Sometime after midnight I dropped into a dreamless sleep.

The next morning I woke with an idea. Miss Penny wasn't exactly the goose that laid the golden egg, but chickens and their eggs were a rare commodity. By noon I'd sold two lovely brown eggs for two dollars each to a lady who wanted to bake a cake for her daughter's wedding. That left me with two more eggs in my basket. Perhaps it was premature, but it gave me a guarded sense of optimism.

Sheriff Longstreet stepped out of the saloon and strode my way. Despite the heat, he was dressed in black, silver spurs with Spanish rowels jangling with every stride, a gun prominently displayed at his hip.

Longstreet had blown into Dry Rock the previous year, running unopposed for the position that had cost the last sheriff his life. When asked about his background his story changed with every telling. When he purchased a horse whose price far exceeded his meager salary, people began to talk.

I shaded my eyes from the sun that reflected off the silver conchos on his hat.

'I heard about Rolf,' he said. 'Tough break.'

'News certainly travels fast.'

'He should have stayed back in Wisconsin where he belonged. He was out of his element here.'

'I'm afraid that epiphany comes a little too late.'

Longstreet had eyes of gun-metal grey, narrow slits from squinting into an unforgiving sun.

He took me in from head to toe in a way intended to make me uncomfortable. It did.

I saw Lee setting crates of vegetables in front of the store. When he saw the distress on my face he dropped what he was doing and walked over.

'Good afternoon, Miss Coyne, Sheriff.'

Longstreet gave a stiff nod. 'You're just the man I want to see,' he said. 'I'm looking for a girl called White Jade.'

'I haven't seen her,' said Lee. 'I don't

frequent that side of town.'

'How noble of you. I hear Quan Dock has been trying to buy out her contract.'

'You have been misinformed. My brother does not traffic in children.'

'Certainly you know something. There are only so many places to hide in a town like this.'

'Idle gossip does not interest me,' said Lee.

Faced with Lee's impenetrable wall of non-information, Longstreet's demeanor shifted. I could almost smell the bad blood between them. If the sheriff had been a bull he'd be pawing the dust in frustration.

'You know,' said Longstreet, 'there's talk of moving all you Chinamen to the far side of Dry Creek, in which case I might be willing to take the store off your hands if the price is right.'

'Your ambitions are somewhat over-blown,' said Lee. 'I suggest you stick to your side of the street and I'll stick to mine.'

'We shall see. You best get back to your vegetables. I have a matter of importance to discuss with Mrs. Kraus,' he said dismissively.

'I'm Miss Coyne now that Rolf is gone,' I said. 'And I'd like Mr. Lee to stay and bear witness to what you have to say.'

'Miss Coyne,' he said, rubbing his whiskers. 'I like the ring of it. It shows a desire to move on from your current dilemma.' With the conchos flashing in my eyes it was hard to read his expression.

'You presume a great deal for someone who barely knows me,' I said.

'I've heard you Irish girls — even the ones in rags — have high opinions of themselves.' Longstreet snapped a match to life with his thumbnail and lighted a cheroot, the smoke settling under the brim of his hat. 'You might not feel so cocky when your tent is three feet deep in snow,' he said, the cheroot clamped tightly between his teeth. 'I've simply come to offer you employment at the Last Chance. Sooner or later you're going to have to do something to keep the wolf from the door. There's not much work to be had by women in a place like this. The saloon is warm in winter. You can sleep all day if you want to. Right now I'm stuck with half-a-dozen leather-skinned half-breeds. A year or two above stairs and you might say the blush is off the rose.'

He looked at me expectantly as he waited for my reply.

I could feel the angry heat rising from Lee's skin.

'Thanks for the offer,' I said. 'I think I'll hang on to my bloom a while longer.'

'I could pay you twice what I pay those — '

'You have the lady's answer,' said Lee. 'Isn't Isadore Dunne capable of doing his own pimping these days?' he enquired, referring to the owner of the Last Chance.

Longstreet twitched a half smile. 'I'm afraid you're behind the times. Old Izzie is on his way to Santa Cruz. You're looking at the new owner of the Last Chance. In case that son of his decides to raise a stink, I have a legal contract to prove it.'

'That's news to me,' said Lee. 'Izzie told me just last week that he had a new piano coming by wagon freight. That doesn't sound like a man who's preparing to sell out.'

'Let's just say he drew a bad hand at poker.' Longstreet turned his attention back to me. 'And you, Miss Coyne, would be wise to consider my offer. With that soft white skin and — '

The sheriff reached out and ran a lock of my hair through his fingers. I was so stunned I froze.

'Gold silk,' he whispered, in a way that sent a chill up my spine. Lee grabbed my arm and pulled me beyond Longstreet's reach. He was ready to throw a punch, when I touched his arm in a cautionary gesture. There's nothing Longstreet would have liked better than to gun Lee down in the street and take possession of his thriving little store.

'Looks like you'd rather take up with a dirty Chinaman,' he said. 'Too bad his days are numbered in Dry Rock.'

Longstreet looked as if he were about to leave, then turned back and picked an egg out of my basket. He rolled it thoughtfully in his hand, then let it drop to the ground and shatter.

'Oops!' he said. 'Delicate little things, aren't they? You know Susan, the only thing that stands between you and a crib above the saloon is a scrawny chicken and two — make that one — lonely egg.'

He walked away, spurs jangling against the wooden boardwalk, sun flashing from the conchos on his hat band.

'Are you all right?' said Lee.

'I will be as soon as I catch my breath. I doubt we've seen the last of him.'

Lee smiled at me. 'You'll be fine. Longstreet is the only man I've known who can strut standing still.'

We shared a moment of subdued laughter and I already felt better.

'Come. I think we can both use a cup of tea.'

'That would be lovely.'

'By the way, in case you haven't noticed, we're being watched.'

I turned to see a figure looking at us from the second story window of the saloon. It was Lucita Gomez, although I didn't recognize her at first glance. I was shocked at her appearance. She'd lost a great deal of weight since Rolf and I had last been to Dry Rock. The once luminously beautiful girl pressed her palm against the pane as if to impart a greeting, then turned from the window and let the curtain drop. I turned away, deeply saddened.

Lee put the 'Out To Lunch' sign on the door. He pulled the shades against the brutal onslaught of the sun and the interior of the store took on a soft amber glow. Using the top of the pickle barrel as a table we sipped jasmine tea and ate almond cookies. Red paper lanterns with gold tassels hung from the ceiling and the aroma of exotic spices hung in the air. Lee and I shared a comfortable closeness, made more meaningful by the introduction of a common adversary — Sheriff Longstreet.

I admired Lee's strength of character and calm self-assurance. For the first time since I'd arrived on the frontier I didn't feel lonely, abandoned, hungry or cold.

'Lee,' I said. 'What do you think really happened to Izzie?'

'The same thing that happened to Lum Tan.'

'I've never heard that name.'

'You wouldn't have. He ran the cribs of Chinese girls on the other side of Dry Creek until someone put a bullet behind his ear. White Jade was his youngest and most beautiful pleasure girl, a painted doll with tiny bound feet that he reserved for his most wealthy clientele. When Lum Tan was murdered, Longstreet abducted the other girls, but White Jade escaped.'

'Why would a girl choose such a life?'

'They seldom have the power to choose. Some are kidnapped from China, like White Jade. Others are sold into slavery by poor parents. Most, however, indenture themselves in exchange for passage to America, the place they call Gold Mountain.'

'Indenture themselves for how long?'

'Eight years would not be uncommon, although most of them never see freedom. They are often worked from the age of thirteen. They are used up by fifteen and usually dead by their early twenties of disease and neglect. A pregnancy adds one year to their contract. If they run away and are captured, they are bound for life.'

'I find that shocking. You'd think there

would be a law to protect them.'

'Even where there is law, Chinese aren't allowed to press charges or testify in court.' Lee set down his cup and took my hand in both of his. 'Let's not talk of unpleasant things. I don't want you to worry about me. I can take care of myself, and I can take care of you too.'

'I'm not really your responsibility, Lee.'

'We share a water barrel. Correct?'

'Well, yes.'

'In my culture that makes me responsible for your well-being.'

I laugh softly. 'I don't believe you.'

'I made it up, but I will make it true.'

* * *

When I returned to the tent I kicked off my shoes, let Miss Penny out to forage, and collapsed on the nest of quilts, the stress of the day having overtaken me. I felt something hard against my hip and tossed back the coverlet. It was Rolf's gun — same crooked barrel — same loose chamber. Where did it come from? What did it mean?

I stepped outside, the hard-packed earth hot on the soles of my feet. I saw nothing unusual — children playing — dogs sleeping in the shade — riders trotting down the rutted street.

I saw movement from the corner of my eye and looked up. Lucita was looking down at me from a second-story window of the saloon. The petite Mexican girl with the snapping dark eyes looked old and worn. My mind drew a parallel to the Chinese girls trapped in the cribs — one life as hopeless and brutal as the other.

I lay my hand over my heart in silent friendship, and she returned my gesture with a plaintive smile. She suddenly leaned over the sill and etched the shape of a star on the air. She pointed her finger and pantomimed a gun. It took a moment to grasp her meaning. The sheriff, the man who wore the star, had killed my husband and taken the gun that Lucita had returned to me.

A dark form appeared behind her. Lucita was jerked back from the sill and the window was slammed down by a heavy hand.

My speculations led me to one conclusion. Rolf had not been murdered for a paltry dusting of gold, but for me, his wife. Once I was unprotected, hungry and cold, Sheriff Longstreet assumed I would be easy pickings. He did not know me. I had already survived the arduous trip west, the hardships of Lost Horse Creek, and the Great Hunger that had swept Ireland. I would somehow survive this too.

Where I was born, auburn hair and green eyes were as common as daisies in the grass, nothing special at all. But here in the southwest, where darker skins were the norm, I could be a real money-maker for the Last Chance Saloon. I, however, had other plans for my life. I just didn't know what they were yet.

Longstreet preyed on helpless women and young girls, but who could I complain to? It was simply the reality in uncivilized places. It was survival of the fittest and the most violent.

I returned to the store and told Lee what I'd learned. At least we had the gun. It was flimsy evidence of murder, but we placed it in the safe at the assay office for safekeeping.

* * *

Deep in the night I woke to the sound of weeping. I pushed the tent flap aside and stepped into a heavy mist that had settled low over the town. A big blurry moon floated over the rooftops and for once the saloon was quiet, the patrons either passed out or gone home.

A green lantern flame flickered uncertainly in the access alley behind the Last Chance. A man with a big square head and a nose the size of a ship's rudder was unloading seven or eight trembling Chinese girls from a barred cage on the back of a horse-drawn cart. When the smallest among them began to wail, Square-head backhanded her and the others went silent. He rushed them up the back stairs to the cribs and the night went suddenly quiet as if nothing had transpired. I wondered if the little runaway was among them.

As I turned toward the tent, a wavering

candle flame appeared in Lee's upstairs window. A shadow moved across the window shade, then two images melted into one. I dropped my eyes and went back inside, a small flicker of hope extinguishing like a candle flame.

Lee had come to mean more to me than I should have allowed in the short span we'd known one another. I thought I'd sensed a connection between us, a slight visceral tug. The more I thought about it, the more I understood my place in the natural order of things. Why should a successful merchant be interested in a girl who sold chicken eggs in front of a tent? I smiled, albeit a bit sadly, but I was a girl acquainted with the realities of the world.

The next morning I put on my blue calico dress, arranged my hair in a long braid down my back and set myself on course. There was a big brown egg in the straw and I sold the last two in my basket to the preacher's wife. As she walked away, the eagerly awaited freight wagon pulled in front of the saloon and the town came to life.

Jasper French jumped down from the wagon seat and commenced watering his six sweaty mules. Longstreet stepped out of the saloon and the men engaged in a heated argument. The sheriff shoved a piece of paper into Jasper's hand and stomped back into the saloon.

A feisty black terrier began nipping at the legs of the mules. After a kick sent him rolling in the dust, he chased a cat up a pole. I gathered up Miss Penny, placed her in her box inside the tent, and tied down the flap.

After Jasper cooled down his mules, he pulled the wagon in front of the general store. Lee waved me over and the three of us went inside. We settled in chairs around the wood stove and Lee gave us each a bottle of sarsaparilla.

Jasper was as done-in as his team. He took his hat off and rolled a cigarette. He was a tough, sun-pickled mule skinner who delivered goods to the far-flung outposts of the west. He had been shot by bandits, porcupined with Apache arrows and had never lost a shipment. To the delight of local youngsters, he often displayed his multitude of scars and even let them feel the arrowhead embedded somewhere north of his liver.

'So, what's going on at the Last Chance?' said Jasper. 'I'll be damned if I'm going to turn Izzie's piano over to Sheriff Longstreet. It's bought and paid for, and if it goes to anyone, I figure his son is next in line.'

Lee told Jasper the story that Longstreet was telling everyone in town.

'That's a crock,' said Jasper, scraping a match on the stove and lighting a cigarette. 'The only place Izzie is headed is Boot Hill. I found him lying in a gully twenty miles east of town with two bullets at the base of his skull. His son Alvie and the undertaker are on their way there now.'

'Longstreet had his eye on the saloon. Now he has his eye on my store,' said Lee.

'What was the paper Longstreet was waving in your face?' I asked.

'The transfer of title to the saloon. He thinks he's entitled to the piano as well.'

'Did the document look genuine?'

asked Lee, leaning forward in his chair.

'I suggest you take a look,' said Jasper. 'It was signed by Dunne all right, but instead of Isadore Markham Dunne, he signed it *I.M. Done*.'

Lee and I looked at one another in disbelief.

'That would never hold up in a court of law,' I said. 'It was obviously coerced.'

'What court?' said Jasper. 'The circuit judge won't be back in Dry Rock for another six months, provided he don't get scalped along the way.'

'Then we'd better come up with a plan of our own,' said Lee. 'If you can get hold of Alvie, we can meet back here tonight and mull this over.'

'We got ourselves a deal,' said Jasper. 'In the meantime, there's a great big piano blocking access to your delivery.'

'Let's move it into my storage room for now,' said Lee.

The piano came in a sturdy wooden crate, and I got out of the way while the men wrestled it into one of the two back rooms of the store. Jasper helped unload the wagon and after he left to bed down the mules at the livery stable, I stayed to help stock the shelves with the new merchandise. There was coffee, flour, sugar, tobacco, whiskey, patent medicine, hard candy, bolts of calico, prospector's tools, guns, ammo, lanterns, tents, boots, rain slickers and everything else a person needed in a small frontier town. It was all very exciting.

Eager customers poured through the door and I found myself measuring cloth, bagging vegetables and filling orders. By the time the crowd thinned and we closed for lunch we were in high spirits. I tucked a stray wisp of hair behind my ear and brushed dust from my sleeves.

'That was fun,' I said, 'a bit tiring, but fun.'

'Here comes your reward,' said Lee.

A boy from the Chinese restaurant delivered steaming bowls of vegetables, rice, noodles and delicious seasoned meat in a woven basket. Lee paid the boy. We feasted around the pickle barrel, then settled back with cups of jasmine tea, the steam as fragrant as a flower garden.

Lee sat back in his chair.

'I couldn't have managed without your help today. It was a stampede. It's like Christmas when the freight wagon arrives. It can be months between deliveries.'

'It was fun. By the way, you must call me Susan. Miss Coyne is far too formal, being that we're next-door neighbors.'

He inclined his head. 'Susan, then. It's a nice name. What does it mean?'

'You will only laugh when I tell you. It means graceful. When my mother named me she didn't know how many times I would fall out of the pony cart or off the log into the creek.'

'I think it suits you just fine. Did you know that I was married when I was just a boy?'

'No, I hadn't heard that.'

'It was a long time ago. We were only together for a year when my wife died giving birth to a stillborn son.'

'That is a very sad story, Lee. I'm so sorry.'

'I am not asking for sympathy. Time has dulled the sharper edges of pain.' He leaned forward and took my hands in his. 'I'd long been resigned to living the life of a bachelor and one day dying with no family of my own. Then a pretty girl came to town with an old mule and a pet chicken, and I began to think — maybe — just maybe — '

A shrill scream shattered the stillness. Then came a second scream and the sound of people running down the boardwalk. We pushed back our chairs and rushed through the door into the harsh sunlight, expecting to see a child run over by a buckboard or gunfighters squaring off in the street.

I heard a man say, 'It's that Mexican whore who used to be such a beauty.'

A crowd had gathered in the vacant lot. Every horrified eye was focused on the side wall of the Last Chance Saloon. A girl was hanging by her neck on a rope strung over the second story windowsill.

'Look,' said a woman in a flowered straw hat. 'Someone's chopped off her hair.'

'Oh my God!' I said to Lee. 'It's Lucita.'

The girl's feet twitched. Her body jerked a couple of times and one of her shoes fell twenty feet to the ground.

I stifled a sharp cry.

'Come inside,' said Lee. 'There's nothing we can do.'

As I turned I glanced at my tent. Something wasn't right. The tent flap was open and some of my more delicate items of clothing were scattered in the dust. I rushed over with Lee right behind me.

Miss Penny lay motionless in her box. I picked her up and her head fell to the side, her neck broken, a shattered egg lying in the straw.

'Old Tom!' I cried, running from the tent, Miss Penny still warm in my arms. When I saw the mule nonchalantly nibbling at a clump of sage at the back of the lot, I let out an agonized wail of relief and dropped to my knees.

Slowly, Lee eased me back to my feet and waved over three Chinese boys who'd gathered at the edge of the crowd. He barked something in Mandarin and handed each boy a coin with a square hole stamped in the center. Lee reached for Miss Penny. I clung to her a moment longer and felt her warmth against my cheek. My tears dampened her feathers.

'It's alright,' said Lee, gently taking her from my arms. He handed her to the thinnest little boy, who turned and ran in the direction of Dry Creek.

The second boy led Old Tom down the street to the livery stable where he would be safe, at least for the time being. At Lee's demand the third boy took a wheelbarrow from behind the store and wheeled my possessions into one of the rooms at the back of the store. There was no doubt in my mind who had orchestrated this atrocity. I was overwhelmed with impotent rage.

Longstreet stood on the boardwalk, shoulder to shoulder with Square-head, whom I later learned was named Rasmus. They were watching me, smiling, whispering conspiratorially behind their black cheroots. Longstreet gave me an amused smirk and pointed a finger at me as if he were sighting down on a deer.

Rasmus grabbed his own throat, tilted his head to the side and let his tongue dangle from his mouth as he watched Lucita being pulled back up through the window by one of Longstreet's lackeys. Finding the dead weight too cumbersome to pull inside the window, a knife appeared and the rope was severed. Lucita hit the ground like a discarded bag of laundry, where she would remain until the undertaker arrived. A young Chinese woman stole down the back stairs of the saloon with a blanket and covered the lifeless body.

'Come,' said Lee. 'This is done to break you down. Don't let them win.'

The noonday sun beat down relentlessly. I felt dizzy and sick to my stomach. Even then I didn't want Longstreet thinking I was shattered and helpless. With quivering knees I took Lee's arm; and, walking straight-backed with head high, I climbed the steps and entered the store. I collapsed as soon as the door closed behind me.

Lee caught me and carried me into the back storage room where the piano was kept, and where he sometimes napped at lunchtime. He laid me on a cot at the foot of a large stand-up safe. Along the walls were stacked boxes of merchandise. He removed my shoes and brought me a glass of water.

'If you help me, he'll get back at you,' I said. 'I should give in before someone else gets killed.'

'You will see more clearly after you rest a while.'

'What if he burns down your store?'

'He's evil, but he's not that crazy. If the store goes, the whole town burns with it. There's not enough water in these parts to tame a glass of whiskey, let alone put out a fire.'

Lee left, and returned with a small glass of emerald liquid from his apothecary.

'Here. This will make you drowsy,'

'Absinthe?'

'No. An elixir. When translated, it means 'Sleep Like Death',' he said. 'It's harmless. Mothers give it to fussy children at bedtime.'

'Do they ever wake up?'

'That is a joke, right?'

'Yes, that is a joke.'

Lee left the room so I could rest. I set the elixir on top of the safe, deciding I'd take it only if needed. As I lay my head on the pillow, I heard soft footsteps coming from the apartment above the store. Lee might not have a wife, but he certainly had a secret. I was asleep before I had a chance to give it much thought.

* * *

It was dark beyond the window when I woke to the murmur of voices. Lee, Jasper, and Izzie's son Alvie entered the room.

'Feeling better?' asked Lee.

'Yes. Much better, thank you.' I stood and smoothed the wrinkles from my skirt. 'Hello, Alvie. I'm so sorry to hear about your father.'

'Thank you, ma'am. At least we got to him before the coyotes did. He's back home in Dry Rock where he belongs. Now it's time to put Longstreet where he belongs.'

Alvie was only twenty-three, but twenty-three was a lot older in Indian country than it is back east. Here, you grow up fast, and sometimes not at all.

Alvie often worked at his father's side, was good with people and money, and more than capable of running the saloon if he could only get it back.

The men began ripping into the piano crate with claw hammers and crowbars until the lid was off and the piano stood alone in all its polished glory.

'Wouldn't it be easier to move the piano if you left it in the box?' I asked.

'It's part of a plan,' said Jasper. 'Now, the trick is getting Longstreet over here.'

'You mean to the store?' I asked.

'Yup! Once we get him here, we plan to jump him using the piano as bait. He wants that piano real bad. It'll bring in more customers, and more customers will pay for more drinks and more girls. It's the only one in two hundred square miles.'

'I can get him here,' I said, after giving the plan some thought.

'You?' said Lee. 'That's not a good idea.'

'That's right,' said Alvie. 'We don't want you in the middle of things.'

'I've been in the middle of something all my life. Now, please, air out the cigarette smoke and only leave one lantern burning. I'll never get Longstreet over here unless he thinks I'm alone. Jasper, give me the bill of lading . . . '

We agreed on a plan, and I had every confidence that it would work.

* * *

I carried my lantern through the windy, moonless night. The first chill of autumn was in the air. When I entered the saloon, every man who wasn't too drunk to lift his head removed his hat, not unusual in a town where there was one woman to every hundred men. The bar was uncharacteristically still: men slumped over their drinks; the Mexican girls subdued and red-eyed; Lum Tan's girls huddled defensively in a corner, clinging to one another for comfort.

Longstreet pushed back from the poker table and strode toward me, those beautiful Spanish spurs jangling on the wood floor, eyes like cold grey stones. I spoke before he had a chance to open his mouth.

'Awfully quiet for a Saturday night,' I said. 'Funny how a murdered whore can put a damper on things, not to mention the bullets you pumped into Izzie Dunne and my husband Rolf.'

It was so quiet you could hear a nickel hit the floor.

'You better watch your mouth, lady,' he said, tilting his head to the side like a fighting cock.

'I wonder if anyone did a background check before they voted you into office. I bet you could be tracked by the bodies you left along your route.'

Heads were turning our way. People were listening, people who had liked Lucita and Izzie, and wondered what the real story was.

A customer within earshot gave Longstreet a dead-eyed stare and walked out. Two more men tossed back the remainder of their drinks and followed him out the swinging door.

'You come here to start trouble?' said Longstreet. 'Or maybe you've come to fill the recent vacancy. The offer still stands.'

'I'm not that hungry yet. We'll see what

happens when winter comes,' I said. 'In the meantime, I have a message from Alfie Dunne.'

'I'm sure you do, but his old man signed the saloon over to me, and there's nothing more to be said.'

'He's aware of that; but without the saloon he has no further need of a piano, since he doesn't know how to play it. You can pick it up tonight from Lee's store. In exchange, we want a peaceful town. No more bullets in the back. No more forcing women into upstairs employment.'

'Sure, why not? There's enough go willingly.'

'It has to be gone by the time Lee returns from the other side of Dry Creek. You have one minute to decide, then I'm leaving.'

'There's no deal unless I get the bill of lading. I want everything nice and legal.'

I removed it from my pocket, unfolded it and handed it over.

'That makes it official,' I said.

'Okay, bring it over.'

'Delivery isn't part of the deal.'

Longstreet motioned to Rasmus, who

was sitting at the far end of the bar. He finished his drink and lumbered over.

'Come on,' he said. 'We have a piano to move.'

* * *

The wind was moaning around the corner of the building when we entered through the back of the store.

'There's the piano,' I said. 'The crate stays.'

'Looks like she's shacking up with the Chinese,' said Rasmus, glancing at the cot.

Longstreet snorted a laugh. 'I've never stood in line behind a slant-eye before.'

I was stoic. I refused to let him bait me.

'There's a furniture dolly in the storage room. It's out the back door to your left. It's behind a pile of crates, but you look like a strong fellow,' I said. 'You can use it, but we expect it back first thing in the morning.'

'Get it,' said Longstreet. 'And take your time,' he said, looking me up and down like I was a side of beef and he was about to order the most tender cut.

Of course, I was scared. This was a turn of events I wasn't prepared for.

After Rasmus left the room, Longstreet noticed the emerald liquid on top of the safe. Golden light from my lantern danced along the rim of the shot glass.

'Open the safe,' he said.

I set the lantern on a stack of crates.

'Why would I have the combination to someone else's safe?'

'Don't play innocent with me, Susan. It's obvious you're playing the Chinaman for a fool.'

'You would think that.'

'You know, from the first time you came to town with that creamy skin and golden-red hair, you were all I could think about night and day.'

I didn't reply. I watched his eyes drift to the glass of green liquid again.

'That's absinthe, isn't it?' he said.

'It's something else. Chinese medicine of some sort.'

'You're lying. I can't even get absinthe for my private stock. Maybe Lee can tell me how he does it.'

'He's resourceful.'

There was a thud and a few sputtered expletives from the adjacent storeroom. My heart was beating fast. Rasmus was not going down without a fight.

'You clumsy ox!' I called out. 'You break something, you pay for it.'

'Where's the gun?' Longstreet asked. 'I want that gun, the one Lucita stole from me.'

'You mean the one you took off my husband's dead body after you killed him? The townspeople are through with you. I'd start looking for your next job is I were you.'

I watched his eyes. They kept wandering to the shimmering emerald liquid. No longer able to resist, he grabbed the shot glass and downed the concoction in a single gulp. His grin turned to a grimace. The taste wasn't at all what he'd expected.

'What the hell is that?' he asked 'Are you trying to poison me?'

'It's called Sleep Like Death. It's some Chinese concoction. Harmless, I'm told.'

He grabbed my throat and forced a bitter kiss on my lips. I bit him on the lip and drew blood. He jerked away and cocked a fist, but as he was about to strike his arm dropped to his side and his eyes lost focus. His tongue thickened as he tried to speak. His eyes rolled into his head. Just as Lee and the men came back into the room, Longstreet's knees unhinged and he thumped to the floor with a jangling of spurs.

'Susan, are you alright?'

'I am now.'

'What did you do to him?'

'Nothing. He drank your potion. You guys took long enough.'

'The man was an ox. He didn't go down easily.'

Lee looked at Longstreet. 'He must have been allergic.' Lee felt a pulse in his neck. 'He's alive, but he won't stay unconscious forever. We'll have to work fast.'

Jasper and Alvie dragged Rasmus's body into the room.

'He weighs a ton,' said Alvie. 'I think he swallowed an anvil.'

The men laughed and hefted him off the floor. One, two, three, and they flung him into the piano crate. Then, without a word, they scooped up the lighter Longstreet and dropped him on top of his henchman. Within moments they had the lid securely nailed down and loaded into the back of the freight wagon. Lee and I watched as the wagon disappeared in the darkness.

Back inside the store, Lee picked up a broom and tapped on the ceiling with the handle.

A door opened at the top of the interior staircase. Velvety footfalls descended the stairs.

Before my eyes stood the most exquisite little creature I'd ever seen. Her eyes were demurely cast downward, her shiny black hair tumbling over her shoulders. She was dressed in white silk brocade, tiny beaded slippers on her bound feet.

'Susan, I'd like you to meet my thirteen-year-old niece, White Jade. She was kidnapped from the house of my elder brother in Shantou, China. Now that she is free, she will be living with Quan Dock and his wife.'

* * *

The next morning, Lee and the Chinese boys delivered the piano to the Last Chance Saloon, where Alvie soon hired an old black man from New Orleans who had more luck with a piano than he had panning for gold.

The Chinese girls were sent to San Francisco to find suitable husbands. Some of the Mexican girls went back home. Others were content to remain now that Alfie had his father's saloon back.

As soon as Lee and I had a moment to ourselves, we tracked down a Buddhist holy man and tied the knot.

* * *

At high noon, Jasper French pulled his team up to a two-hundred-foot drop in the Badlands of Apache country.

Longstreet had been a damn disruption — cursing, begging, kicking at the inside of the crate — for the last twenty miles, his silver spurs jangling. Jasper couldn't really blame him, being stuffed in a hot box with a dead man. He only wished he'd had the foresight to remove those fancy Spanish spurs before they nailed down the lid.

He backed the wagon to the edge of the gorge and considered pumping a few bullets into the crate before he sent it tumbling into space. It would certainly be the civilized thing to do. Then again, Longstreet wasn't a civilized man and this wasn't a civilized country. He fingered the arrowhead embedded beneath his skin, and decided he might just need his ammunition for a more worthy cause, like saving his own hide.

Jasper climbed in the back of his wagon. It took all of his wiry strength to inch the crate along until gravity finished the job. He watched the crate somersault end over end until it was the size of a die and disappeared into the chaparral at the bottom of the gorge.

Of course, someone would stumble onto it — eventually. An Indian looking for a lost sheep, or a bandit running from the law. It could happen tomorrow. Then again, it might not happen for a hundred years.

In time, he'd forget Longstreet's face.

He'd even forget his name. But he'd never forget leaving behind them fancy silver spurs.

Bruised

The digital clock read 3.00 a.m. when the phone jangled me out of a drug-induced sleep. Reaching for the receiver, I cursed as I banged my bad knee on the nightstand. Mom's brogue was as thick as potato soup in my ear.

'It's Rory,' she said, softly rolling her Rs.

At the mention of my diminutive twenty-one-year-old sister with her flying red hair and out-of-control lifestyle, the pain in my shattered knee went into overdrive. Now what? A drunk-and-disorderly? Another DUI?

'I don't need this,' I croaked through a haze of painkillers.

'She's missing, Joey. And she's pregnant.' I squinted as I snapped on the bedside lamp and threw a t-shirt over the shade to shield my eyes from the glare.

'Tell me a rumor I haven't already heard. I just wished she'd hooked up with a guy from the neighborhood instead of a rich old dandy in silk skivvies.'

'And a coward to boot, slappin' her around so she can't even hide the bruises anymore.' That rumor had been circulating for a while too.

'Listen, Mom, you think Stafford needs his ticket punched, call Pug. He's the muscle in the family.'

I tapped out a Camel and lit it.

'Jesus, Mary and Joseph, you're the cop, Joey.'

'Remember my knee, Mom? The shotgun blast? The doc says I'm off the leg for six weeks or I could lose it.'

'That would never have stopped your dad when he was on the force. Listen to me, boyo, Stafford is facing eighteen years of a rich man's child support. He told Rory he'd have her down at the clinic if he had to drag her by the hair.'

Seemed reasonable to me, drugged up that I was.

'She's a good Catholic girl, Joey.' I rolled my eyes. 'This morning she went to have it out with Mr. Moneybags. No way she could go to the clinic on Friday and face Mick at Sunday Mass. Stafford says she never showed up at his place.'

'I suppose you called the clinic.'

'They never heard of her. Worse yet, she hasn't showed up at The Emerald Isle all night.'

Not showing up at her favorite haunt on a Saturday night? Maybe this was more serious than I thought.

'I'm thinking he's done her in this time. Rumors about this guy go back to when your dad was walking the beat.'

I rubbed my temples as the tumblers fell into place with an ominous click.

'Go back to bed, Mom. I'll look into it.'

I pinched out my smoke and burned my thumb. The ashtray tumbled to the floor. It was going to be one of those nights. I rubbed the ashes into the grey shag with my foot. Perfect match.

* * *

Like a 1930s movie star, Colby Stafford lounged in the doorway of his upscale townhouse in a burgundy silk smoking jacket, a teenage blonde with a black eye draped like a wilted daffodil over his arm.

He was fiftyish, clean-shaven and cologned. If you looked close enough you could see sins crawling beneath his skin like tropical parasites.

'Oh God, Fannon McFeeney has sent one of her boys to check on Little Sister,' he said.

He lit a lavender cigarette with a gold filter and made a point of not inviting me in, even though I listed starboard on my cane. With a twitch of impatience he shrugged the girl away and she vanished with a pout.

'You got lucky it's just me standing here,' I said. 'Mom was ready to take my dad's old service revolver and blow your shit from here to kingdom come.'

'You get the same answer she did. I haven't seen Rory in days.'

I glimpsed something in the foyer, and when I limped past him he didn't stop me. I grabbed a red leather purse off the entry table. Back on the stoop I discovered Rory's personal items inside.

'Want to try again?' I said.

Stafford gave a world-weary sigh. 'So I told a little fib to keep things on an even keel. She kneed me in the groin when she found Tiffany in my bed, then left in a manic frenzy. It was last night. About ten.' That didn't jive with Mom's account, but I let it ride. 'She's the poster girl for ADD. Enough of her crap. I'm moving on.'

'Now that you have her in the family way? How inconvenient for you.'

'Get real. Could be me or one of a dozen others.'

He might be right, but I still wanted to bust his face.

'Ever heard of DNA?' I said, handing him my card. He examined it gingerly with well-manicured fingertips.

'Lieutenant? I'm impressed. You're moving up in the world.'

'Call me if your memory improves. My home phone's on the back.'

As he turned the card over I saw a fresh cut on the back of his knuckles, the kind you get when you punch someone in the mouth and catch an incisor for your trouble.

'Mind if I come in and look around before I'm on my way?'

'Got a warrant? If you're on active duty with that gimp, I'm Peter Pan.'

'Got something to hide?' He blew a perfect smoke ring toward the porch light. 'How did you cut your hand?' He blanked for a second, then plastered a tight smile on his kisser.

'That little nick? Tiffany talks back, but she's young enough to learn.'

'My sister was born talking back. She'll never learn.' We locked eyes. This time he didn't waver. 'Just one more question and I'll get out of your hair. When Rory left here, was it under her own steam or inside a suitcase?'

I landed on my bad knee at the bottom of the steps before I saw his fist move. A howl ripped from my throat. I moved my bottom jaw to make sure it was still attached to my face. The door slammed and the porch light went out.

I had to give it to him. Mr. Fancy Pants packed an iron punch. I struggled awkwardly to my feet. In my dad's day I could have kicked the door in and shot him where he stood, but it was hard to get away with that brand of justice anymore. Officially, I was on leave, home in bed recuperating. I couldn't justify my presence at Stafford's to the chief. Payback would have to wait.

As I hobbled to my car, a neighbor stuck his head out of a second-story window. 'Shut the hell up or I'm calling the cops,' he yelled, and slammed the window back down.

* * *

A cold rain fell as I drove down the strip where the bars had gone dark. Fluid ballooned my knee to surreal proportions. I looked for Rory's car. I peered down dark alleys. The damp cold crept into my bones. The only signs of life were a dog raiding a garbage can, and an old guy sleeping it off in the entryway of an all-night cafeteria.

When I got home I collapsed in my easy chair with a brandy and examined Rory's purse. Someone had wiped blood from the leather, but it had soaked into the stitching and collected deep in the crevices. But was it Rory's blood?

Stafford's? Tiffany's? How long had it been there? What did it prove? Only a forensics lab could answer those questions. As I was mulling things over, my brother Pug called.

'Mom's been driving me nuts all night,' he said.

'Tell me about it. I'm getting the same treatment.'

'One of Vin's boys found Rory's car out by the old slaughterhouse with a flat tire. There was blood on the steering wheel, her phone in the mud, but no sign of her. They checked the abandoned buildings but came up empty.'

'That's interesting, being as she's never owned a cell phone. Did you press redial?'

'I tried, but it's dead.' He cracked his knuckles. 'I brought Mom up to date. God forgive me, but growing up with Rory was like being trapped in an outhouse with a hive of bees. You can't get no peace.'

'You're a real poet, Pug. I ever tell you that?' I related my encounter with Stafford, told him about the purse and the blood, the torn knuckles and the black-eyed blonde.

Pug, my younger brother, owns The Aces High, a front for his gambling operations and other stuff I don't want to know about. Mick, my older brother, is a parish priest at St. Brigit's. I followed Dad into The Job. He took a bullet in the back a week before retirement — typical family in Little Ireland east of the factories. If you're Irish, you know that even in your happiest moment, misery is just around the next corner. It's a curse that runs like a dark humor in the blood.

I was in agony, out of pain pills, and my knee so swollen it wouldn't bend. As dawn broke with a rumble of thunder, I dragged into Doctors On Duty on my way across town. An MD who looked like a high-school student drained a liter of suspicious fluid off the joint with a needle the size of a garden hose. He gave me an ominous look, like in the movies when the doc is about to saw your leg off.

He went to the phone. 'Who's your doctor of record?'

'My what?'

'Your primary physician.'

'I'd rather not say. Look, Doc, I just

need more pain pills.'

'Not from me,' he said. 'You're staying off this leg, right?'

'Absolutely.'

* * *

Vinnie Natoli was sitting at a table with Pug. He hadn't missed many meals since I saw him last.

'Well, if it ain't Quasimodo,' he said, squinting through a toxic cloud of cigar smoke as I hobbled in and eased painfully into a chair around the card table. 'We heard about the kid with the shotgun.'

'He could have been me at seventeen,' I said. 'I can't get that out of my head. It was like lookin' in the freakin' mirror. I almost started down the same dead end when my old man got his ticket cancelled.' I shifted in the chair and leaned my cane against the table.

'Maybe so,' said Vin, 'but you never would have iced the clerk at the Likkor Lokker. Glad you smoked him. He had it coming.'

'It didn't go down that way, Vin. I was

flat on my face in the parking lot, my knee already blown out. My partner dropped him with one clean shot through the left eye.'

Vin roared. 'You mean Deborah Moskawitz saved your sorry ass? She used to beat me up and steal my lunch money in fifth grade. I shoulda known back then she had the makings of a good cop.'

After Vin wound down, Pug poured us a round of eye-openers. I tossed mine back and thumped Rory's purse on the table next to the cell phone Vin had brought from the slaughterhouse. Rain hammered the roof above our heads. I shot Pug a quick look, and he caught my meaning. What the hell was Vin doing here? Why was a goomba brought in on family business?

Pug poured me another shot. It helped take the edge off the pain in my knee.

'Vin's got a stake in this too,' said Pug. 'Tell him the story, Vin.'

Vin downed his shot and said, 'Guess who my cousin Angie was involved with when she dropped off the face of the earth?'

'Stafford,' I said. I knew the conversation was about to turn down a dark alley. Vin wasn't laughing anymore. I lit a smoke and gave him my full attention.

'He hit her so hard she went deaf in one ear,' he said. 'She threatened to file a complaint, and disappeared on her way to the courthouse. She was sixteen, for Chrissake. She'll always be sixteen. That was seven years ago. We never recovered so much as a tooth. That's how gone she was. We put up a gravestone for my Aunt Marie, but there wasn't nothing under it but dirt.' Vin's eyes were melancholy, dark as Italian olives. 'And she ain't the only girl dropped down the same black hole. You find so much as Rory's fingernail, you'll be the first to find anything.'

'I ran his name last month,' I said. 'Didn't come up with zilch.'

'That's no surprise. He's the biggest contributor to Supervisor Wright's campaigns. The charges disappear. The missing girls go on the books as runaways. Stafford always picks 'em young, a little wild, usually estranged from their families, so when they ain't around no more, no one digs too deep.'

Pug's knuckles went off like firecrackers in a coffee can, a habit he's had since he was a high-strung kid. Made me wish he'd start smoking again and quit with the knuckles.

'We don't close this guy down, no one will,' said Pug.

Even if I trusted the veracity of Vin's account, I was apprehensive at being sucked into the vortex of their reality. I liked to think that I was removed, if only by a hair's breadth, from the world of thugs, gamblers, and goombas. I groaned and rubbed my tired eyes.

'Let's slow down a minute,' I said. 'Things are going a little too fast for me here. No need to go off half-cocked.'

'What, slow down while he runs off to the Bahamas, like he's done before?' said Vin.

Who knew? Maybe they were right. 'Stafford will be on guard, especially after our little tête-à-tête,' I said. 'He knows I'm coming for him sooner or later.'

Vin hunched forward conspiratorially. 'Every Saturday night at nine sharp, my nephew Gino picks up Stafford and drives him to the Carnival Room across the river. Tonight he's putting the limo at your disposal. Do whatcha gotta do, just don't leave no evidence behind.'

I downed another shot and took a Trappist moment to clear my head.

Vin threw his arms in the air. 'Stop worrying! It'll be dark and stormy. He'll never see it coming.'

I reluctantly nodded assent. Pug poured another round. This time I felt the burn in my empty stomach.

Vin grew pensive. Ever since we were kids he was subject to sweeping changes of mood.

'Rory was the prettiest girl at St. Brigit's. The only one brave enough to sass the nuns,' he said. 'She knew how to stick up for herself, and how to stick it to anyone who crossed her. I worshipped her. Why do you think she never gave me a tumble?'

'She had a reputation for picking the wrong guys,' said Pug. 'Be happy you dodged the bullet.'

When Vin rolled out the door and

pulled away from the curb in his pink '48 Caddy, he had a smile wrapped around his fat cigar.

Rain rattled on the roof and Pug set an ashtray on the pool table where a leak had broken through.

'We're going to have our hands full with Stafford,' he said. 'He might seem prissy as hell, but he's an iron fist in a velvet glove.'

'Tell me about it,' I said, moving my jaw to see if it still worked.

'I say we get Mick to drive while we take care of the business end.'

I slowly stubbed out my smoke.

'I hate to get a priest mixed up in this mess,' I said.

'So we should use Vin? And he calls up the favor down the road, wants somebody bumped off, wants us to smuggle a little dope?'

I threw my arms in the air. 'Okay, you're right. Best we clean up our own side of the street.'

I called the rectory at St. Brigit's and woke up Mrs. Duffy, the housekeeper. I heard her slippered feet pad down the hall to Mick's room.

'Father McFeeney,' she called. 'It's trouble on the phone.'

He moaned sleepily and pulled himself out of bed.

'Pug or Joey?' he asked.

* * *

When night came the streets were flooded, shingles flying off rooftops and fallen branches littering the roads. Mick looked the part of a limo driver in his priestly casuals and Gino's shiny-brimmed driver's cap. His nose was flat as a boxer's and his round Irish face as knuckly as a fist. There wasn't a wife-beater or gang-banger he hadn't dumped on his butt.

He let me and Pug off a block up from Stafford's townhouse, and circled back to make the pickup. I desperately wanted to ditch the cane, but couldn't navigate without it. My face burned with fever, the fluid had built up in my knee again, and I felt a vague disconnect from my surroundings.

Pug looked down the road and saw the

limo coming our way. 'The bastard fell for it,' he said, rain pouring from the brim of his cap. Mick pulled to the curb and splashed us from the knees down. I plopped clumsily in the back seat on the driver's side, and punched my gun into Stafford's ribs. Pug opened the opposite door, and there sat the teenage blonde. Whoops!

Pug didn't miss a beat. He reached into his wallet, pressed a fifty into Tiffany's hand, and left her sputtering on the street corner with rain dripping into her shiny high heels. I didn't like the idea of a witness, but there was no turning back.

'What the hell?' said Stafford, looking first at me, then at Mick. 'Where's Gino? Where the hell is Gino?'

'Just relax,' said Pug. 'We're going for a little ride.'

'If this is about Rory, I already told you — '

'We can make it about her . . . or, let's see, we can make it about Angie Milano.'

Bull's-eye! He turned my favorite shade of corpse grey, and I knew that everything Vin had told us was true. We'd probably never see our sister alive again.

'I didn't think you Irish mugs hung with the Eyetyes,' he said. 'They were born talking trash. You're spinning your wheels. You can throw me in jail but my lawyer will have me out by morning. You got nothing to go on.' As he thought things through, a bit of color crept back into his face.

'He thinks we're bringing him to the station,' said Mick, tossing his clerical collar onto the seat beside him. Mick, Pug and I laughed and laughed, like when we were kids in the shadow of the factories and up to no good.

'No body. No crime,' said Pug. 'Is that what you tell Mrs. Milano when she leaves flowers at their daughter's empty grave?'

Stafford went silent and the miles slipped by.

We drove beyond the city lights to a marsh along the river where an abandoned fish cannery rotted along the bank. We stopped and exited the limo. Stafford walked quietly now, caged in by three Irish mesomorphs with murder on their minds. I was trembling with fever, my knee barely supporting my weight. Pug gave me a concerned look and relieved me of my gun before I accidentally shot myself.

The floorboards of the old cannery were mushy with rot. I shone my flashlight into the watery abyss twenty feet below where a section of floor had fallen into the river.

'Let's get the job done and get the hell out of here,' said Pug.

Mick turned to Stafford. 'For the sake of your soul, clear your conscience and tell us where the girls' bodies are buried.'

'You unmitigated hypocrite,' said Stafford, a tear in the corner of one eye.

The building trembled in the wind and my eyes wandered back to the hole. Water sloshed back and forth on the rocks below.

Quick as a rattlesnake, Stafford's hard-soled shoe sank into the soft, swollen pulp of my bad knee. I shrieked like a banshee and my flashlight tumbled end over end into the black water below. Then, with a sickening crunch that sounded like the breaking of giant bones, Stafford plummeted downward through the rotten floor into the abyss.

'Holy Mother of God!' gasped Mick. 'We didn't need the gun after all.'

No sound or movement came from the bottom of the hole, just the ghostly glow from my flashlight shining beneath the water.

'We're outta here,' said Pug, pocketing my piece.

'I can't walk,' I said. My brothers grabbed my arms and dragged me none too tenderly to the limo. I'd become unaware of my agonal vocalizing until Mick said, 'Stop with the moaning. What would Dad say if he heard you whimpering like a little girl?'

Later that night in the ER, Dr. Irvine chewed me out in royal fashion. 'Don't bother telling me how it happened,' he said. 'You need a keeper, not a doctor.'

* * *

The next morning, I lay in bed with a knee the size of a watermelon. When I heard someone try the doorknob, then kick in the front door, I hoped they'd come to shoot me and put me out of my misery. A pain shot across my chest when

Rory flew into the bedroom, an unstable fire burning in her eyes, three stitches decorating her upper lip. She turned to me, hands on hips.

'Well, and if it isn't you malingerin' when you ought to be at Sunday Mass. You might have gotten your lazy butt out of bed and let me in.' She saw her purse on the chair and slung the strap over her shoulder. 'Pug told me you were in possession of my purse. I hope you've had fun snooping through my things.'

The voice that thundered out of me would have put Caruso to shame. 'WE THOUGHT YOU WERE DEAD! Mom's been out of her mind with the worry of it all.'

'Then the old battleaxe should keep her nose out of my business. Leave it to her to make all those embarrassing inquiries as to my whereabouts.' She looked him up and down. 'It doesn't look like you were all that worried, makin' the most of your wee injury. If Dad were alive — '

'Well, he's not. Where have you been?'

'I finally got the nerve to get in Stafford's face. We fought. I got the worst of it, but I had my say. I took off — none too sober, I admit — hit a curb, blew a tire. This kind young doctor from St. Elizabeth's came along. He stitched my lip and put me up for the night. Poor man lost his cell phone in the mud. Anyway, he asked me to move in with him, so I'm off to pack my things. I've got nothing better to do at the moment.'

'Wait a minute! What about the baby?'

'You worry too much,' she said, and with that she was gone.

I was beginning to get a grip on myself, maybe finding a little humor in the situation. After all, we could always use a doctor in the family.

The phone rang. I picked up. It was Chief Dunning.

'I had the weirdest experience about an hour ago,' he said. 'Your sister's rich boyfriend paid us a visit with mud all over his nice cashmere overcoat. He says he was kidnapped by a gangster, a cop and a priest, and that they tried to murder him down by the old cannery. When that little blonde he keeps on the side wouldn't back up his story, we laughed him out of the station and sent her back to her parents in Topeka. Ever hear a more ridiculous accusation?'

My mouth went dry. I swallowed hard. 'No. Never.'

'By the way, how's Father Mick?'

'Fine.'

'And your brother Pug over at The Aces High?'

'Couldn't be better, Chief.'

'And yourself?'

'Still resting in bed like the doctor ordered.'

'Well, me boyo, I suggest you stay there and give us all a rest.'

Bullets in the Rain

Berlin, Germany

One a.m. and the lights burned dimly in the offices of Wolfenburg and Zimmerman, Diamond Brokers.

'This better be important,' said Saul Zimmerman, 'getting an old man out of bed at this hour.'

'Hymie Rosenbloom has vanished,' said Arthur Wolfenburg. 'This is the third disappearance on Diamond Row in the last week.'

Saul shrugged. 'So, three fewer competitors is a bad thing?'

'This is no joking matter.'

'They've probably taken their diamonds to Amsterdam for cutting, same place I'll be next week.'

'There may not be a next week. Don't you see what's happening? The *Geheime Staatspolizei* are bumping us off one by one. They want to steal our fortunes to back the Reich.'

Saul threw his arms in the air. 'Such drama! I fought on the side of the Fatherland in the big war. I have decorations to prove my loyalty.'

'We are Jews. That's all that matters to them now. Katie and I are leaving the country tonight. Come with us, Saul. Please.'

The old widower straightened his yarmulke. 'I'm too old to start over.' He peered at Arthur over his spectacles. 'I suppose you want I should buy you out just like that?'

Arthur looked at his watch. 'I'll take my half of the diamonds. The business you may keep. *Mazel tov,* dear friend.' He kissed Saul on both cheeks and squeezed his wrinkled hand.

Arthur watched from the upstairs window as Saul walked into the deserted street, leaning heavily on his cane. Five men stepped out of the shadows, their truncheons raining down on the old man's head. Arthur would always remember that one shrill cry as Saul crumpled into the gutter, his life bleeding out on the wet cobbles.

Arthur ran to the safe, his hands shaking. He emptied great handfuls of diamonds and family heirlooms into a purple velvet bag and stuffed it in his overcoat. As he fled down the back stairs to the alley, Hitler's goons crashed through the front door, their boots thundering up the stairs to his office.

Arthur and his grown daughter Katerina caught the midnight train to Paris. A week later they bordered the *Empress Josephine* for America. By then, every headline in Europe read: *Diamond Broker Arthur Wolfenburg Murders Partner and Flees With Stolen Millions.* At that moment Arthur and Kate found their life's mission, to get as many Jews out of Europe as they could — while there was still time.

Santa Paulina, California, USA

It was pouring rain when I left my car in the back alley and headed toward Duffy's speakeasy. Even in the dark I couldn't miss the hot yellow Caddy parked next to my geriatric coupe. It certainly didn't belong to anyone I rubbed shoulders with.

The speak was under the protection of Duff's brother, Lieutenant Pat Connor, who made sure he got a healthy cut of the take. They admitted high rollers like Mayor Bristol and miscellaneous riffraff like me, PI and repo man Pete Draeger.

Duff slid a gimlet across the bar when he saw me coming. I shook the rain from my fedora and unbuttoned the neck of my trench coat.

'Prohibition, and now the Depression,' I said, popping an olive in my mouth and downing a reverent slug of gin. 'First they take our booze. Next it'll be our cigarettes.'

'Hasn't slowed you down any, Pete.'

'They just busted Sam's Place down by the river. You have anything to do with that?'

Duff poured himself a shot

'He doesn't have a brother on the force, poor chap. Besides, his stills have lead fittings that leaked into the booze. Three of his customers went blind. Two died. You peddle bootleg booze, it's gotta be clean.'

'I can't argue with that. How is my good friend Pat these days?'

'Crooked as ever, thank God — but in a nice way,' he said, smiling.

He ran a cloth over the bar. When he looked up, he said, 'Get a load of that,' and nodded behind me into the room.

I did a slow turn. A stunning long-haired brunette with ivory skin and tears floating in her blue eyes sat at a table against the far wall. A stocky guy in a brown suit with his back to me was giving the lady a hard time. Even from behind, he looked vaguely familiar. Duff leaned forward on his elbows and spoke in a low voice.

'The lady is the former Katerina Wolfenburg. Her old man took a dive off The Saticoy penthouse last month.'

'You don't mean Arthur Wolfenburg?'

'The same. I hear the son-in-law tapped him for everything from bar bills to gambling debts. You can see how hubby is handling his reversal of fortune.'

Brown Suit grabbed the lady's alligator

purse, and when she hung on to the strap he gave her arm a nasty jerk. She batted the fat cigar from his mouth and he tossed a glass of champagne in her face. A few people gasped. He looked around and realized he was the focus of whispers and finger-pointing. He let go of the purse, but only after he dug out a roll of cash from it. He stuffed his pockets and straight-armed out the door. I caught a glimpse of his face in profile.

'Holy crap!' I said.

'You know that guy?' asked Duff.

'That's my boss. What the hell is a millionaire's daughter doing with a caveman like Barney Troyer? I had the impression he was single.'

'Maybe that's why the lady has filed for divorce. I hear he has memory lapses regarding his marital status.'

I tossed back the rest of my gimlet.

'I'm looking at an empty chair,' said Duff. 'So is that guy sitting alone in the corner, and he's a heck of a lot better-looking than you are.'

While Good-Looking was pondering his next move, I walked across the room and folded my six-foot frame into the chair Barney had vacated. I handed the lady a clean handkerchief from my inner breast pocket. She accepted it without a word. She wore a classy raincoat — the kind you see on London streets — alligator shoes to match the purse, and a silk turquoise scarf looped casually around her coat collar.

'Is he always that nice, or is this a special occasion?'

'You should see him behind closed doors,' she said, her wet blue eyes studying my face. 'He's just getting warmed up for the main event.'

'I'm Pete Draeger,' I said.

'Kate.'

She dabbed lightly at her face and handed the handkerchief back to me. It was damp with champagne and the scent of gardenia perfume. I folded it and slipped it back in my pocket. I took her gloved hand in mine and gave it a comforting squeeze, careful not to hold it as long as I wanted to.

'So, Pete, what do you do when you're not drinking bootleg booze?' she said, recovering her composure.

'Trying to keep the wolf from the door like everyone else.' I had no intention of telling her I was her soon-to-be-ex-husband's repo man. I offered her a Chesterfield. Her soft hair cascaded over her shoulder as she leaned forward for a light. She saw me glance at her unadorned left hand.

'The rings?' she said. 'He ripped them off my finger when I filed for divorce. Funny thing is, they weren't from him. They'd been my mother's, a ruby ensemble with a scattering of diamonds.' Kate had a pleasant accent, the kind that comes from years in a Swiss boarding school, a far cry from my education in the school of hard knocks.

'You needn't feel sorry for me, Pete. I knew from the start what I was getting into. There was no way to avoid it at the time. Barney is just being Barney.' She quietly worked on her cigarette, tucked a lock of hair out of her eyes. 'I'm sure the Depression is part of it. Business is bad. I read where the African Cameroons sent Hoover $3.77 to *Help the starving Americans*.'

'Then Hoover has the nerve to tell us that people are leaving their jobs to sell apples on street corners because it pays better. Better than what? The nonexistent jobs?'

'Better Hoover than Hitler.' She butted out her smoke and touched her purse like a child might touch a teddy bear. 'My father gave me this for my last birthday. I never dreamed it would be the object of a wrestling match.' She looked up. 'Barney has no doubt taken my Cadillac and left me without a ride. Mr. Draeger, would you be so kind as to call me a cab?'

'I'll be even kinder. Come on, I'll give you a lift. Duffy can attest to my sterling character.'

'Oh, I can see you're a character, Mr. Draeger.'

'Try Pete.'

'All right. Pete.'

'Drop me at The Saticoy if you would. Home might not be my best option tonight.'

I slipped a five under the candle for Duff. It was a lot of money back then when two bits got you a hot lunch at the diner, and a fin hooked you up with two-and-a-half willing ladies at The Sleepy Eye Motel.

I nodded to Duff. He smiled at me and we left.

Rain blew in horizontal sheets, lightning X-raying the weary bones of the city. Water poured off the brim of my fedora and glittered like silver beads in Kate's hair.

'You're going to a lot of trouble for a stranger.' She smiled, ducking into the collar of her coat. Laughing, we dashed across the parking lot, trying to avoid the larger puddles.

'I love trouble,' I joked. Especially when it was soft and curvy and smelled like the ghost of gardenias. I took her hand and we walked the rest of the way to the coupé.

We got as far as the passenger-side door when we got paddy-whacked by two dark figures that came out of nowhere. Kate fell hard onto her knees and a fist came down like a sledgehammer on the back of my neck, my fall broken when my forehead cracked against the front fender.

One of the mugs grabbed Kate by the hair and threw her into the back seat of a waiting sedan, her startled scream muted by the wind. I was staggering to my feet when the Rock of Gibraltar landed on my head.

I reentered consciousness in a shallow puddle with a lump on my head the size of a grapefruit. I'd never seen the weasel-faced bum who'd cold-cocked me, but I'd recognized Renzler, one of Troyer's lackeys. Together they blackmailed the cheating spouses they were hired to follow, collecting on both ends of the same deal, loyal to no one but their wallets. Dull fellow that I was, I stuck to repos. I didn't cheat anyone. I simply consigned them to public transportation.

I dragged myself into the coupé, seeing double and suppressing an urge to throw up my gimlet. Whatever quack said the brain is incapable of feeling pain had never been inside my head. I'd driven a mile before I realized I'd never make it home before passing out or driving head-on into a lamppost. I pulled into a lot behind a Chinese restaurant and staggered the rest of the way to the Rutger Building. The clock in the lobby read 2:30. Except for the grinding of the ancient elevator that carried me to the third floor, you could have heard a pin drop on the dark side of the moon.

TROYER DISCREET INVESTIGATIONS was stenciled in black letters on the pebbled glass door. I used my key and walked through Barney's larger office to my smaller one via a door on the right.

Rain battered the window behind my desk, blurring the pink and gold lights from the movie marque across the street. There was a small private washroom through a door on the far wall. I had a coat closet, hat rack, file cabinet, and a typewriter plagued by misspelled words. A clutter of active files sat next to the phone and a black leather couch stood against the wall opposite the window. I spent many nights here when I worked late. No one waited for me back at the flat — no wife — no cat — not even a houseplant.

I wobbled to the washroom and threw up in the toilet — gimlet, olive and all.

The walls spun and a hamster wheel turned in my stomach. Mismatched pupils looked back at me from the mirror above the sink — all four of them. I took three steps, collapsed on the couch and sank into oblivion.

It was the sound of the elevator rattling to the lobby and back up again that woke me hours later. When it bounced to a stop and the grate rolled open, I heard Barney's coarse laughter and a trill of female giggles. It wasn't Kate. She wasn't the giggling type.

Renzler may or may not have recognized me in the dark alley. Either way, if Barney saw me in my present condition, he might make the connection between me and Kate and the speakeasy. I eased myself from the couch, head banging with pain. By the time his key clicked in the outer door, I was inside my closet. Being an inquisitive sort I left the door open a crack. I heard stumbling, muffled voices, a few thumps against the wall.

'Come on, baby. There's a couch in Draeger's office. He's been gone for hours.'

My couch? Thanks one hell of a lot.

They opened the door to my private office, came in and made themselves at home. A fluffy-headed blonde clung to Barney's arm. He snapped on my green-glass desk lamp and elongated shadows stretched across the walls and ceiling.

The girl might have been pretty if she hadn't had enough lipstick on her mouth to paint a barn door. She raised her arms playfully and he slipped her pink angora sweater over her head. He began fumbling with the hooks and eyes of her bra.

'Did you get me the alligator purse?' she asked, her voice all warm and syrupy.

He nibbled at her throat. 'It didn't work out this time, Peg.'

I almost laughed out loud. This was a better show than the one playing across the street.

'Barn, how could you let me down like this?' she whined.

'I got nothing to hold over her head now that the old man's gone. I'll get you a nice replica.'

'A phony? That's not what you promised. It has to be *the* purse. Barney, you're not listening!'

'Okay, okay, I'll snag it next time, Buttercup.'

He turned her to the wall to work on the last stubborn hook. She swung back around and thumped his chest with her hand. Surprised, he stumbled back a step.

'You seem to get pretty much everything you want,' she said, the syrup in her voice hardening to peanut brittle. 'And since we're on the subject, what about the engagement ring you promised me?'

'I've already ordered it. It's a five-carat ruby set in a circle of diamonds.'

I rolled my eyes. The only ring she'd ever get from old Barn was the one around her bath tub.

Peg reached behind her back, nimbly fastened the hooks, then slipped her sweater back over her head. 'Let me know when you can put it on my finger — Buttercup!'

Barney clenched his jaw and tugged roughly at her sweater. She just as roughly slapped him in the head. She straightened her skirt and headed for the door.

'Where are you going? You can't leave me like this.'

Her high heels clicked across the marble hall to the elevator.

'Peggy, for God's sake, be reasonable!'

I heard the elevator rattle downward. Barney punched the couch and kicked the wastebasket against the far wall. Temper, temper!

The phone rang and sent a bolt of pain through my head. Barney stomped off and took it in his office.

'Troyer here,' he barked. I eased out of the closet and listened in on my desk phone. There was a telltale click on the line, and I held my breath.

'Hear that? Someone's listening.' It was Renzler's voice.

'You idiot,' said Barney. 'It's the storm screwing with the lines. Did you get the jewelry?'

'Yes. It was in the bottom of her purse. We busted her up a little like you said, made it look like a random mugging.'

'She's not an idiot, you fool. I'm the only enemy she has. It's late. I'm going home to exercise my marital prerogative. Be here tomorrow night, eight sharp. One piece of glitz goes missing, I'll boil you in your own slime. By the way, did you get the purse?'

Renzler snickered.

'Sorry, Boss. I didn't know you swung that way.'

'It's for Peg, you moron!'

'Hey Boss, you still thinking about that insurance thing? Unless you make up your mind, Pyco is flying out as soon as he gets paid for tonight.'

'Don't freakin' crowd me. I'll make up my mind in a day or two.'

Pyco was a name I hadn't heard before. If Troyer was using outside muscle he was up to something big.

'By the way, she had some tall bozo with her,' said Renzler.

'Probably that rich Jew lawyer of hers.'

I was relieved. Renzler hadn't recognised me.

'Who knows? Pyco cold-cocked him with a sock of billiard balls.'

They both got a good chuckle out of that. No wonder I was seeing double. I was lucky to be alive.

'Gotta go,' said Barney.

He slammed down the receiver, snapped

off the overhead and left.

I hung up the phone. That was quite an earful.

What insurance thing? With the divorce pending, Kate might be worth more dead than alive. I doubted he'd torch his own house. Troyer, Renzler and Pyco were not that hard to figure — greedy bottom-feeders out for an easy buck. But Kate marrying a Neanderthal like Troyer? That was a mystery. Whatever Troyer held over her head had to be big.

Now that I had the office to myself I tossed it, starting with my own desk. It had to look like a garden-variety break-in. Then I pillaged Barney's. Top desk drawer. Saturday night special. Loaded. I took it along with his address book and his infamous little black book. That should make interesting reading. At the back of the drawer I found the ruby-and-diamond rings.

Sorry, Peg.

I wrapped my wool muffler around my fist and drove it through the glass door as I made my exit. I retrieved my car and reached my flat as the garbage truck rolled down Cole Street.

When I woke mid-afternoon my pupils were once again as closely matched as snake eyes on dice, but the pain was still there. I swallowed three aspirin with black coffee and put the rings in my pocket. Knowing Barney would be at the office, I headed to the Troyer house on Whippet Run.

As I neared the two-story Tudor, the yellow Caddy was pulling out of the driveway with Kate at the wheel. She wore a red raincoat with a matching hat and sunglasses that failed to hide her bruised cheekbone. Curious, I hung back and followed her from a distance. She drove a few miles east and parked in front of the Southern Pacific Railway Terminal. I pulled into an adjacent lot and watched her go inside.

Two cigarettes later she came out shepherding three men in tall black hats and full beards, a woman wearing a flowered babushka, and two small boys. I followed her back uptown through the rainy streets, my windshield wipers clicking like metronomes. An attendant parked the car and Kate ushered her strange flock of crows into the lobby of The Saticoy.

I double-parked and made a mad dash past the doorman in time to see the elevator float upward to the penthouse. I walked through the thickly carpeted lobby, reached into my pocket and handed the concierge the rings.

'Please see that Miss Wolfenburg gets these,' I said. He sputtered as I headed toward the revolving doors.

'Sir!' he called. 'Whom shall I say these are from?'

I thought a moment. 'Tell her Speak-easy Pete is watching her back.'

I felt like an idiot the moment I said it. Famous last words from a guy she last saw lying facedown in the gutter.

* * *

Peggy had been so furious with Barney that she spent the night with Franco Gallante. Served him right for being such a horse's behind. Franco was a gorgeous Italian mobster. Among other enterprises, he owned the strip club where she danced. He had pale green eyes and skin like Etruscan gold. He was certainly hotter in the sack than old Barn. The roll of twenties he left under the pillow was so fat that only half of it fit in her wallet. Now, that was how a gentleman is supposed to treat a lady.

Peg could not stop obsessing over the alligator purse. Now she could buy one of her own — but it wouldn't be the same. Kate's purse represented the value Arthur Wolfenburg had placed on the relationship with his beautiful daughter. Peg's own dad — well, Mom said he was her dad — denied ever having met her mom, and if he had, he'd been too drunk to remember.

More and more, Peg thought of dumping Barney. Then she reminded herself that the rich, educated Katerina had married him. Beneath his crude exterior there must be virtues that evaded the unsophisticated eye.

The roll of cash was heavy in Peg's purse. She had never once gone into a store with enough money to buy everything she wanted. She walked up and down every aisle, trying to decide where to begin.

A nice clerk in Ladies' Apparel helped Peg make her selections: a tailored navy-blue suit with a white silk blouse, a beige raincoat, soft kid gloves and a graceful black umbrella. She went on to buy bags and bags of classy accessories. She went from Macy's to Cute Cuts and turned her brassy blonde fluff into a sunny brown bob, her lipstick from fire-engine red to a soft peach. Now she looked like any other lady who had tea at the Garden Club.

That evening she stood in front of her bedroom mirror, thrilled with the results. All she needed now was Katerina's alligator purse, and someone to love her like Mr. Wolfenburg had loved his daughter.

* * *

The curious secretaries who had been standing outside Barney's ruined door scurried back to their offices when he stepped off the elevator. He cursed as he crunched to his desk through the broken glass.

Who the hell would have the nerve to cross Barney Troyer? Clients he'd ripped off? There were too many to count. Friends he'd scammed? Lowlifes he'd blackmailed and roughed up? Men whose wives he'd seduced? Or — Peg!

The rings were gone. Hadn't she stomped out of the office, mad about the purse, mad about the rings, mad about everything? Alright, she had a point. He'd led her on, made a lot of promises in the sack he never intended to keep. That was what guys did. It wasn't like she hadn't been around the block more times than the Fuller Brush man. She knew how the world worked.

Barney lit a cigar and got a grip. He'd survive without most of the stolen items. He'd replace the gun. He didn't much care about the address book. But the black book? That could put him behind bars if it fell into the wrong hands, which apparently it had. What if Peg gave it to that greasy boss of hers? Franco would have the power to take over his whole operation. At least she'd left his bottle of whiskey and his expensive cigars.

He poured a shot and rested his oversized head in his hands. His father-in-law had made life easy until he took that selfish swan dive off the penthouse roof. Now his finances were in the toilet, and his gambling debts were a mountain he could no longer climb. As for his creditors? They weren't the kind of people you crossed.

* * *

I hid the gun in my sock drawer and spent the rest of the day going over the items I stole from Barney's desk. Nothing in the address book raised a red flag. The black book, however, was a detailed account of blackmail, arson, assault, rip-offs, loan sharking, people he owed money to and people who owed him. My, oh my! Barney was a busy boy. As I leafed through the book a newspaper clipping from a European paper drifted from between the pages.

DIAMOND BROKER ARTHUR
WOLFENBURG MURDERS

PARTNER AND FLEES WITH STOLEN MILLIONS.

How the hell had Barney come by this article?

A theory began to take form. If Barney had threatened to have Arthur deported to Nazi Germany it would be a death sentence, even if the charges weren't true.

Arthur Wolfenburg was not the subject of a murder plot. His suicide was a willful act. Barney would never have killed the goose who laid the golden egg. He would, however, have used the information in the newspaper to blackmail Kate into marrying him. Arthur had set her free from the bonds of unholy matrimony by sacrificing his life.

* * *

Windblown branches scraped against Peg's upstairs window. She had always been afraid of the dark, especially when she was alone. As she dabbed a few drops of French perfume behind her ears, she heard a tremendous thud. Heavy footsteps thundered up the stairs. She screamed as Barney barreled through the bedroom door.

When she saw who it was she laughed with relief.

'Barney, for God's sake! I thought you were an intruder.'

'What have you done to yourself?' he said.

'I had a makeover. How do you like the new me?'

She whirled in a circle to show off her floaty new lingerie.

'Where's my black book?'

She looked at his angry face and her smile vanished.

'What black book, Barn?'

He grabbed her purse and emptied the contents onto the bed.

'What are you doing?'

'Where's my gun?'

'What's wrong with you, Barney? You know I'm afraid of guns.'

He looked at the fancy purchases that were spread across the bed.

'Where did this stuff come from?'

'Mostly from Macy's.'

'That's not what I mean. I'm talking

about the money.'

'Where do you think? I work. I have a job.'

He grabbed her arm and twisted it behind her back.

'You pawned the rings you stole from my desk.'

She began to cry. 'I don't know what you're talking about. You're breaking my arm.'

'Don't lie to me.' He spun her around and grabbed her face in his giant hands. 'How else could you afford all this?'

'Go to hell!' she screamed.

The last thing she remembered was his fist coming at her like a sledgehammer. An hour later, when she regained consciousness, she didn't recognize herself in the mirror. She picked up the phone. She was going to call the police, but at the last minute she changed her mind.

'Franco, it's Peg.' She broke into ragged sobs. 'Barney just tried to kill me. My face is all busted up.'

* * *

Barney left Peg's in such a rage he thought he was going blind. He drove for fifteen minutes before his heart stopped jackhammering. He could tell after a few minutes that Peg had nothing to do with the break-in, but by then he was all wound up. He thought of the way she'd frozen him out the other night and figured she deserved what she got. Besides, she was a nobody, just some dame who danced for money.

* * *

At dusk I drove through the rain looking for Pat Connor, Duffy's brother. I found him having dinner at The Greasy Spoon. He was ruggedly handsome in his blue uniform — silver crewcut — rock-solid frame. I slid in the booth across from him and the waitress brought me coffee.

'What, you need a ticket fixed or something?' he said.

'It's more like *or something*.' I set the black book next to his cup.

He flipped through it with growing interest. I told him about Barney and

Renzler cooking up some kind of insurance scheme, and asked if he'd heard the name Pyco before.

'Sounds like Jackie Pyco, a hit man out of Chicago. His brother is a councilman so nothing they throw at him sticks.'

'I bet it would stick if he got busted here. I think his target is Kate Wolfenburg, Barney's soon-to-be-ex-wife.' I continued to fill him in on everything I'd heard. I told him I wanted Kate protected.

'Did he target her by name?'

'Not exactly, but it's got to be her.'

'I need something more concrete in order to move on it.'

'What, you want her on a cold slab to prove she's in danger?'

'I want you back in that closet when the three bozos are together. See what else you can find out. Then get back to me.'

'You got it.' I drank my coffee halfway down. 'I want the book back,' I told him.

'Maybe, when I'm through reading it,' he said, putting it in his breast pocket.

I didn't argue. He was bigger. He had a gun. I left the rest of my coffee and slid out of the booth.

'One more thing, Pete. Try not to get yourself killed.'

* * *

The following night I beat Barney to the office by fifteen minutes and was dutifully hunkered down in the closet by the time he settled in his chair and poured a shot. I heard Renzler enter the room with the weasel-faced Pyco. I felt vulnerable and idiotic, like a kid hiding from his old man behind his mom's coat. I held a highball glass to the wall to amplify the conversation in the next room. I'd have felt better if the glass was filled with Scotch.

'What the hell happened to the door?' asked Renzler, looking at a patch of cardboard covering the square where the glass had been.

'Normal wear and tear,' grumbled Barney. He slapped the desktop. 'Dump the jewels,' he said.

I heard the jewelry spill out across the desk. The sound conjured images of royal tiaras, handfuls of pearl necklaces, and enough scarlet and blue gems to fill a pirate's chest.

'You're sure it's all here?'

'All of it, Boss.'

Barney lit a cigar. The toxic smoke penetrated my hiding place. Barney said smoke kept the building free of termites. My throat went bitter and dry and I yearned for a glass of anything wet.

'Unless you make up your mind about the hit, I'm flying out tonight,' said Pyco. 'Time is money and I got jobs piling up back in Chicago.'

Hit. The word was finally out. A hit on who? Come on. Say it.

'Don't crowd me,' said Barney. 'First I have to off some of the glitz. Meet me here tomorrow night, same time, and I'll have the cash.'

After they were gone I stood alone at my desk looking at the lights from the movie house. I called Pat and brought him up to speed.

'Now can I get protection for Kate?'

'Come on, Pete. You haven't heard a name yet. A guy like Troyer might have any number of people lined up to take a hit. Maybe his butcher sold him a tough steak. Stay on it one more night. Get something concrete and I'll move on it.'

I waged a brief protest, but the guy was a rock.

'I'll get you out of this as soon as possible,' he said. 'If Troyer can't raise the cash, Pyco goes home and there is no hit. He goes down for the jewels either way, although he might try to claim marital assets. I'm with you, Pete. All I need is a name.'

'Sure, Chief, I'll read it to you off Kate Wolfenburg's toe tag.'

* * *

The next morning Barney walked into Wickersham's, the most reputable jewelry store in this part of the state. He tumbled a glittering array of jewelry onto the counter-top: a diamond-and-emerald ensemble, a glittering sapphire brooch that had belonged to the Romanoffs, weighty handfuls of glamorous, glorious glitz. The take from this caper could keep him in hookers and Cuban cigars till hell froze over.

Mr. Wickersham was already suspicious. Precious jewelry was kept in velvet or satin-lined cases, not poured out onto glass counters, gems rubbing and scratching against one other like Cracker Jack prizes. It was an offense to Wickersham's patrician sensibilities.

Mr. Wickersham put a loupe to his eye and carefully examined each item. He looked up and gave Barney a troubled look of inquiry.

'What is it?' asked Barney. 'These pieces have been handed down through generations of Eastern European nobility.'

Wickersham removed the loupe and raised a delicate eyebrow.

'These are some of the most exquisite replicas I've come across. They are indistinguishable, upon first glance, from the genuine pieces I purchased last week. You must understand, fine ladies keep their high-end jewelry in bank vaults as a security precaution. They wear these to social events where they might be subject to thievery or loss. Without a discerning eye and a jeweler's loupe, no one can tell the difference.'

'You mean these aren't real?'

'Correct. But they are excellently crafted and should be handled with care.'

Barney was suddenly aware of his rumpled coat and scuffed shoes, his nasal hairs and his neglected fingernails. He scooped the phony loot back in the bag and ran from the store. Now he'd have to dig into the money he'd stolen from Kate's purse.

Barney had thought he'd won the Irish Sweepstakes when Renzler crept through the Wolfenburg penthouse and brought him that London newspaper article. It was the perfect blackmail scheme: got him a rich wife until her father jumped off the hotel rooftop and ruined it all.

He climbed in his car and pounded on the steering wheel until his hands began to swell. What could he possibly have done to deserve such bad luck?

Wickersham smiled and stepped away from the window. He walked to the phone and made a courtesy call to the lovely Miss Wolfenburg.

* * *

Kate had just set her alligator purse on the entry table at Whippet Run when the call came in from Mr. Wickersham. She thanked him for keeping her informed and terminated the call. Now that she'd moved back to the penthouse, she dreaded returning to the place where she had been so unhappy. She was tired of being used, and ready to buy her freedom rather than go through a lengthy court battle.

She paced nervously, waiting for Barney's car to come down the street. She'd offered him a generous cash settlement, but he was late as usual. All he had to do was sign the papers in her briefcase and they would both be free.

Tonight she'd been cautious and left what jewelry she hadn't sold in the hotel safe, just a few sentimental pieces her grandmother had left her. Everything else of value — jewelry, paintings, and *objets d'art* — had been sold to help finance the Jewish Rescue Project. A dark wind surfed through the treetops and she felt a growing sense of unease.

★ ★ ★

Barney, Renzler and Pyco came up the elevator and entered the office together. By now I knew the interior of the closet like a prisoner of war knows his cell. The desk chair groaned under Barney's bulk and he lit a cigar. Within moments the toxic smoke had my stomach churning with acid. My nerves were at the breaking point. I'd been living on coffee, aspirin and cigarettes.

'I want the job done now,' said Barney. 'She's at the house and I don't think I can get her alone again after tonight.'

'I want ten thousand upfront, and another ten when the job is done,' said Pyco. 'Renzler drives.'

'That's twice the going rate. Who do you think you're dealing with?'

'I charge ten for a nobody. Katerina Wolfenburg is a somebody. She's high-risk.'

Finally. A name. Katerina Wolfenburg.

'We're in the middle of the Great Depression, remember?' said Barney. 'You think I'm made out of money?'

'Take it or leave it. I don't like being off my home turf.'

His challenge was met with silence. The money just wasn't there.

'He's right,' said Renzler. 'It's risky. He goes down, I go down. I want the same deal. Besides, it's peanuts after you collect the fifty thou from the insurance.'

Barney was so mad he was seeing stars. That stupid SOB and his big mouth. After Kate got hers, Renzler was next.

Pyco smirked. Troyer couldn't control his own flunky's flapping tongue.

Barney turned on Renzler with a dangerous look in his eyes.

'You get a C-note after it's over, provided you don't hit a tree or run over her neighbor's cat. I got a dozen guys can drive better than you.'

Renzler sounded hurt. 'You underestimate me, boss.'

'I sure as hell hope so.'

'I thought you were going to off the jewelry,' said Pyco. 'You were going to be rolling in dough, remember?'

'It didn't work out. They were copies.'

'Those copies are still worth plenty. I'll

take the jewelry upfront, and ten thou after the insurance pays off. If she's the victim of homicide, it's going to be double indemnity.'

Barney opened his bottom desk drawer and handed Pyco the heavy bag of glitz.

'I can pass a lot of this off as genuine,' he said. 'Ready to call it a deal?'

Barney extended his hand. Pyco squeezed it painfully and held on. 'You screw me, you're next.'

Barney turned on the juice and crushed Pyco's knuckles even harder. 'So far the only thing you've shot off is your mouth. Let's see what you can do with a gun.'

'Then let's stop the BS and get down to business,' said Pyco, loosening his grip and shaking the pain out of his fingers.

The highball glass slipped from my sweaty hand. I immediately stopped its roll across the closet floor but I knew they'd heard something. I hunkered deeper into the corner behind the coats. The connecting door between the offices opened. Shoes scuffled around the room. The washroom door opened and closed. They looked in the closet but didn't push the coats aside or look deep in the corner. I heard a little nervous laughter and they closed the door.

'Let's get this over,' said Pyco. 'We're spooking ourselves with all this waiting around.'

Pyco and Renzler finally left but I still heard Barney's chair squeaking. I counted on him leaving with the others, maybe lying low in a motel room for the night. I heard him pour a shot. I smelled another wave of cigar smoke. Seconds ticked by. He might sit here for an hour. I had to call Pat. I had to warn Kate.

I moved stiff-legged from the closet, crept to the connecting door and quietly slid the deadbolt into place. My door had the same frosted glass pane as the one that opened onto the hall, so the bolt wasn't much of a deterrent to someone determined to make entry.

I picked up the phone. Barney hummed away on the other side of the door. The phone number for the house on Whippet Run was written on the back of the business card Barney had given me when I first went to work for him. I dialed it and Kate picked up on the second ring.

'Barney?' she said.

'Kate,' I said, as quietly as possible. 'This is Pete Draeger. Barney's goons are on their way to kill you. Get out of the house now. Just drop everything and go.'

I hung up without waiting for a reply, and dialed Pat, whose number I knew by heart.

'Is somebody in there?' It was Barney. 'Is that you, Pete?'

I heard his chair roll back and nudge the wall.

My heart was pounding. Pat, pick up, pick up, *pick up*!

'Hello.'

'It's Pete. Troyer's goons are on their way to the Troyer house on Whippet Run. Kate's alone. They're going there to kill her, the two of them, Pyco and Renzler. *Go, go, go!*' I slammed down the receiver as Barney tried the door.

'You SOB,' he said. 'What the hell are you up to?'

'You woke me up, Barn. I was just sleeping off a hangover when I heard voices.'

Of course, he didn't believe me. When

they'd searched my room I hadn't been on the couch. He rattled the doorknob once again, then leaned into the door with his beefy shoulder. On the third try the frame shattered and the Marquis of Queensberry rules went out the window. I cold-cocked him as he stumbled over the wreckage. He landed facedown on top of the broken glass and shattered wood. I took the stairs, leaped over the last six feet of bannister, and hit the marble floor at a run.

I fired up the coupé. The tires chirped as I smoked away from the curb and flew toward the fancy suburbs on the north side of town. I peeled into Whippet Run, punching the horn like a madman, trying to draw as much public attention as I could.

The neighborhood was very quiet at this time of night. The black sedan I remembered from the speakeasy was parked at the bottom of Kate's driveway, the barrel of a rifle protruding from the passenger-side window. I heard the sound of sirens coming from the other end of the street.

Kate came running down the driveway, the strap of the alligator purse looped over her shoulder. I did the first thing that came to mind: revved my engine and drove up the trunk of the black sedan. I heard the gun go off as my forehead hit the steering wheel and my head whipped back against the seat. Renzler gunned the sedan but Pat Connor had already blocked him in from the front. Three more squad cars swooped onto the street. Renzler and Pyco bolted but didn't get very far.

I shoved open my car door to the shriek of crumpled metal and ran toward Kate. She took two more gallant steps before she collapsed on the driveway. I raced to her side and gently rolled her on her side. A long dark wig tumbled off her head and rolled away, exposing a short bob of brown curls. The woman with the alligator purse was not Kate, but a gravely wounded Peg. The bullet, however, was less shocking than the devastation I saw on her face. Someone had beaten her almost beyond recognition. I used my tie for a tourniquet and wrapped it above the bullet wound in her arm. Even in her pain she clung obsessively to the purse.

High heels clicked up the driveway from the street as Kate ran from a neighboring house. She knelt down beside me in her red raincoat. When she'd run from the house, she'd left everything behind including her purse. I was relieved to see her in one beautiful piece.

'What's happening, Pete?' she asked, kneeling beside Peg.

'It's complicated. I'll explain later.'

'Who is the girl?'

'Someone who came to steal your purse. Someone your husband knows from — the office. She disguised herself to look like you.'

'Who would want to look like me?'

Just about every woman who came to mind, but I didn't say it.

'My God, what happened to her face?' said Kate.

'I imagine the same thing that happened to yours,' I said, looking at her bruised cheekbone.

Pat Connor trotted up the driveway and joined us. He had a big grin on his face. 'Let's see the councilman get Pyco out of this one,' he said. Rain spun out of the dark sky.

'Kate, this is Lieutenant Patrick Connor.' She nodded.

'If this is Kate, who's that?' he asked, looking at Peg.

'A case of mistaken identity,' I said.

As a patrol car drove away from the scene, Renzler and Pyco were yelling at one another from the back seat. An ambulance wailed up the driveway and the storm ratcheted up a notch.

'I'm riding to the hospital with the girl,' said Kate. 'I want to make sure she gets everything she needs. I'll call you later, Pete,' she added, as she followed the stretcher into the ambulance. I watched the taillights disappear in the distance.

'Let's bust Troyer's balls,' said Pat.

'He's probably in another jurisdiction by now.'

'Let's go find out.'

* * *

We climbed the stairs to the third floor of the Rutger Building. Pat drew his gun as we approached the office. We stood to the side of the door.

'Come on out, Troyer,' called Pat. 'The jig is up.'

No response.

'It's too damn quiet,' I said. 'He's not in there.'

Pat pushed the door with his foot. It slid halfway open. Dead silence. We followed the gun at the end of Pat's arm into the room.

Barney sat at his desk, a fat cigar clenched between his teeth, his nose flattened by my sucker-punch. He still didn't look half as bad as Peg, except he was a lot deader. There was a perfectly centered bullet hole in his forehead. His right hand was frozen in his top desk drawer.

'Looks like he was going for a gun,' said Pat. I thought of Troyer's gun sitting back home in my sock drawer. I knew when to keep my mouth shut. This was one of those times.

'Somebody stole your thunder,' I said. 'You think it was a mob hit?'

'Could be,' he said. 'The shooter was

probably in and out in thirty seconds.'

My thoughts turn to Peg's boyfriend, Franco Gallante — but why implicate someone for hauling out the trash?

I spent the next three weeks recuperating from whiplash. When I went to pay my medical bills with the last of my savings, they'd already been taken care of. There was only one person I knew with that kind of money. Pat came by with a carton of Chesterfields and Duffy with a bottle of gin. Then Katerina called and invited me to the penthouse. A cab was already waiting for me at the curb. The rain was gone. The sun shone for the first time since the last Ice Age.

Kate smiled and invited me inside. 'Lieutenant Connor told me all about you,' she said. 'We all need a hero from time to time, and you are mine.'

'He's a cop. You can't believe a word he says,' I told her, and we both laughed.

She led me across an acre of thick white carpeting to an equally white couch. Her dark hair was shiny and loose around her shoulders, and she looked stunning in a pair of jade silk lounging pajamas.

I wanted to take her out to dinner or a drink at Duffy's. Instead, she introduced me to her fiancé Benjamin Kahn, Attorney at Law. Ben, of course, was young, rich and too handsome for words, although I could think of a few choice ones. When they told me they were slipping back into Germany, I thought they were nuts, being that every sane person was sailing in the other direction.

'We have friends and family who are trapped there,' offered Ben. 'We want to help them secure passage to America, Argentina or Palestine, any place that will have them. We know the risks involved and we're willing to take them on — together.'

We talked over champagne and French pastries. During a lull in the conversation, I said: 'Hear anything about Peggy?' Not that I really cared.

'The small news,' said Kate, 'is that I called a plastic surgeon who reconstructed the damage to her face. The big news is that she's engaged to a charming young businessman named Franco Gallante.'

'Yes, I've heard of him,' I said,

suppressing the urge to elaborate on his finer points of character.

A few days later when I emerged from my flat, a polished yellow Cadillac with spotless whitewall tires was parked at the curb. There was no sign of Kate. I found the registration and keys in my mailbox with a thank-you note: *A small token of gratitude for your kindness and courage. Kate.*

Like all lovesick fools, I'd dreamed that we might spend one stolen night together with soft music playing and rain on the roof. It would have filled my heart for the rest of my life — just one night. Next-best scenario? She leaves me the car of my dreams.

The world changed fast after that. The Eighteenth Amendment was repealed, taking the guilty pleasure out of sneaking off to the speakeasy. Duffy even went legit. The voters kicked Hoover out of the White House, and FDR blew into Washington with new ideas and a war that still raged halfway around the world. Pat was as charming and crooked as ever, and Peggy (who now called herself Margaret) was the wife of the newly elected mayor, Franco Gallante. I could certainly see which way this city was headed.

After orchestrating the flight of dozens of Jewish families from Nazi Germany and occupied Poland, Kate and Ben fell into the hands of the Gestapo. They vanished, along with what was left of the Wolfenburg fortune, and so many other Jews who met the same fate. Some said they were put on a train to Auschwitz-Birkenau, others that they were transported to Treblinka. We'll never know for sure.

I've been running the PI agency for twenty years now, all on the up and up. No more extortion. No strong-arm stuff. California's rainy season is on us again, and a storm batters the window behind my desk.

From the darkness of my office I watch the pink and gold neon from the movie house flicker across the wet asphalt. I pull an old handkerchief from my pocket and hold it against the greying stubble on my cheek. When I close my eyes I see a beautiful dark-haired woman trailing a cloud of gardenia perfume. Laughing and light-hearted, she crosses the landscape of memory.

I lock up and take the elevator down to the street. I climb into an old yellow Cadillac and head home to a flat where no one is waiting — no wife — no cat — not even a houseplant.

Trouble in Gunnar

Mom was barely cold in her grave when Bell Jones began warming Dad's bed. Well, that's not entirely fair, being that Bell was no dummy and first made sure they tied the knot in front of Pastor Blevins, all legal-like.

I told Dad to get one of those prenuptial agreements, like Tom Cruise and Donald Trump. After all, look what happened to Paul McCartney. Dad came into the marriage with a dairy farm and bank accounts, and Bell came with a few faded cotton dresses and a cardboard suitcase she kept under lock and key. Being a kid, and a girl to boot, my opinion didn't carry much weight in the Granger household. Dad ignored my advice and told me I was far too cynical for a ten-year-old.

God knows where Bell came from and how she ended up attending our church. She certainly hadn't grown up in our small community of Gunnar. My big brother Robby and I tried to make the best of a bad situation, but we were terribly lonesome for our real mom, who was pretty and kind-hearted and everything Bell was not.

The week Bell moved in, Robby's dog Kelly was relegated to the barn. Allergies had never been mentioned during the brief courtship, but my cat Sheba was the next family member to be evicted from the house. Mom's picture came down from above the fireplace and Bell's unwelcoming ways drove away our friends.

We complained to Dad but he was smitten. He said we had to make *accommodations;* that it was hard for someone new to fit into a ready-made family. 'It's none too easy for us either,' I said. He told me to watch the sass or he'd wash my mouth out with soap. I wanted to tell him that the soap thing went out with high-button shoes, but I was already in enough trouble.

It wasn't long after Bell moved in that her brother Rafe showed up on our doorstep. Bell was churchy and drab as an old dishrag, but Rafe was hot as a pistol with snapping dark eyes and something of the gypsy about him. I decided to hate him from the get-go just because he and Bell were related, but when she treated him as mean as she treated us, we became best friends. Before the first week was out I had a mad crush on him even though he was twenty years older than me. What the heck, Grandpa Emory was twenty years older than Grandma, and they got along well enough to have six kids.

Rafe had worked as a roustabout for Woodman's Traveling Circus until the operation went belly-up. He was full of adventurous and hair-raising stories of life under the Big Top. It was just the exciting kind of life I dreamed of having someday, with lots of moving around and no two days the same. Dad wasn't sure what he thought of Rafe at first, but when he proved himself knowledgeable about the workings of a farm, Dad let him stay as long as he agreed to bed down in the barn and do his share of the work.

One day, when I was showing Rafe

which cows were easygoing and which ones kicked, Bell flew into the barn and slapped me so hard my ears rang.

'What the hell!' shouted Rafe.

'Don't you dare interfere with my discipline,' said Bell, stabbing a finger so close to Rafe's face that he jumped backward and nearly fell over a bale of hay.

Bell grabbed me by my hair and dragged me up the stairs to my room. A four-fingered welt ran like a red spider across my cheek. My knees trembled. I couldn't imagine what I'd done to deserve this.

'Stay away from Rafe. I don't want you two cooking something up behind my back.'

'I don't know what you mean,' I said. 'I'm telling Dad what you did to me.'

As I tried to push past her she grabbed me by the arm and dug her fingernails in.

'You're not telling anybody anything. You're staying in your room for the rest of the day. You have a splitting headache, do you understand?'

'No, I don't. Dad may think you're the

cat's pajamas, but you don't fool me one bit.'

She got down in my face and said in a whisper: 'Speaking of cats, can you imagine what a microwave could do to that little fleabag of yours?'

After that I shut my mouth.

Robby crept up to my room after dark and I told him everything that had happened.

'I don't know why she hates me so much,' I said.

'She hates you because you're smart. She's afraid you'll figure her out and ruin things.'

'Figure what out?'

'I don't know yet. Something just isn't right about this whole set-up. I'm going to take Kelly and Sheba over to the Hayden farm. Then we'll just have ourselves to worry about.'

Dad put in long days at the farm, but was always with us in the evenings. Bell was all sweetness and light when Dad was around but he didn't see her flip side. We had no television, so we found other way to entertain ourselves. I read aloud from the Harry Potter book I got for my birthday, Dad recited Longfellow poems by heart, and Rafe kept us in stitches with wild tales from his circus days. But Robby was always the star of the show. At fourteen his voice had changed, and through his wooden dummy Jimbo he could mimic the deep voice of a stevedore, the whine of a two-year-old, or the dry cackle of an old lady. Bell, of course, proclaimed ventriloquism as a tool of the devil, and that Harry Potter was written to spread witchcraft.

A week later, Jimbo disappeared and I found poor Harry's ashes in the fireplace. There was a witch in the house, but it wasn't Harry Potter.

In early June, Dad took sick. It scared Robby and me because he didn't smoke or drink or have any bad habits. Now he was plagued with stomach pain, headaches, and general confusion, no longer able to remember things or add long columns of figures. One day he called me Violet, but Violet was his little sister who drowned back in the 60s when they were kids. As time went by he spent more time in bed. This was not normal for a man who'd always been up for the five o'clock milking and still had energy after a full day's work.

We all pitched in with the farm work, tending the cows, gathering the eggs, feeding the animals. Bell seldom left Dad's side with her folk remedies and homemade lentil soup. In The Old Testament, Jacob cured his brother Esau's illness with 'a pottage of lentils,' but Dad only got worse and worse.

Bell prayed and spoke in tongues and placed her faith in the Almighty. She put on quite a show. When Pastor Blevins paid us a visit and saw how yellow Dad's eyes and skin were, he said that God in his grace provided us with doctors, and if she didn't take him to one, he would.

Bell hated anyone who challenged her authority, but she'd finally come up against someone who was her equal. The pastor had a booming voice, and when he said *Jump,* you said *How high?* He spent time behind closed doors talking with Dad. When Bell opened the door, he slammed it shut, and she didn't challenge him a second time.

After Pastor Blevins was gone, and Dad and Bell left for the doctor's office, Robby and I made a beeline for the attic. Jimbo had to be somewhere and we were determined to find him. We rummaged through the attic, kicking up dust and sneezing as we went, but he wasn't there.

'Abby, look what I found!' said Robby. It was Bell's ratty old suitcase that we had strict orders not to touch.

'Quick! Open it,' I said, plopping down on the floor beside him. 'She's been hiding something. Maybe it's money. She's probably been holding out on us.'

The suitcase, of course, was locked, with no key in sight. We tried forcing it open with a hanger but it wasn't flexible enough. We tried a wire but it wasn't strong enough. A bobby pin finally did the trick and the lock popped open. There was no money inside or anything else that looked very interesting. It was a major disappointment until we dug beneath a few threadbare aprons.

I pulled out a red satin dress, a pair of black lace stockings, a curly blonde wig and gold high-heeled sandals. 'Look at this lingerie,' I said, holding up a transparent black nightgown. 'She never wears anything like this for Dad.'

'Look,' said Robby. He pulled a little ribbon and a false bottom opened.

'Holy shit! Look at this,' he said, picking up a small ivory-handled pistol. He cracked it open and found two bullets in the chamber.

As he fooled around with the gun, I pulled out a packet full of documents and saw Bell's face on a dozen driver's licenses. In each one she had different hair color, or a different style or dramatic changes of makeup. In some photos she wore reading glasses, no glasses in others. There were different names to go with the different faces. Belinda Jenson. Bella Johnson. Becky Jackson. The list was dizzying.

'I don't think our new mother is who she pretends to be,' said Robby.

We heard the screen door slam downstairs and frantically pushed everything back in the suitcase and locked it. I hadn't realized how much time we'd spent in the attic.

Robby ran to the window to see if Dad and Bell were back.

'No car,' he said. 'It's got to be Rafe.'

We raced down the stairs to the kitchen and caught Rafe raiding the fridge.

Bell had very strict rules about the kitchen. The fridge and pantry were out of bounds to us peons.

'Busted!' laughed Robby.

'So put me on the Most Wanted List,' grinned Rafe. He was flushed from working in the sun, his hair casually windblown. 'You two look like you've been rolling around in a dust bin.'

'We were in the attic looking for Jimbo,' I said. 'We're not supposed to — '

Robby jabbed me in the ribs and I clamped my mouth shut.

'Find anything interesting?' asked Rafe.

'Not unless you're into dust and spider-webs,' I said, trying to redeem myself.

'Well, if you don't tell on me, I won't tell on you,' he said, stuffing a half-pound of roast beef between two pieces of bread. My stomach growled and Robby laughed.

'She's going to know we've been robbing the fridge,' I said. He shrugged and winked at me.

Rafe cut the sandwich four ways. He took half and Robby and I got a quarter each, which was a lot more satisfying than Bell's skimpy peanut butter and jelly ones.

'If we're going to catch hell anyway, we might as well live it up,' said Rafe.

He set two big mugs of milk on the table, pulled a beer from the pocket of his overalls and popped it open with a hiss.

'Bell would kill you if she saw you bringing liquor into the house,' said Robby.

'Can I have a sip?' I said. 'I just want to see what it tastes like.'

He patted his knee. 'Come sit on my lap.'

'Robby?' he said, holding up the can.

'I'll pass,' he said. My brother gave me a stern look, but I ignored him.

The beer didn't taste all that good, but I liked the way it made me feel. Besides, I loved the sunny warmth of Rafe's skin and his big protective arms around me. Robby and I could use someone on our side.

'I think that's enough,' said Rafe, taking back the can.

'Just one more little sip?' I begged.

'Okay, just one more.'

Robby gave me the evil eye as I pressed the can to my lips and drank far more than I'd planned to. I'd never felt so relaxed and giggly.

'Only eight more years and I'll be eighteen,' I said. 'Grandma was only sixteen when she married Grandpa, and they were decades apart. Some people said it would never work, but it worked long enough to have six kids.'

'That's quite a story,' said Rafe. He gave me a gentle squeeze. 'What do you want to be when you grow up?'

'Why don't we join the circus?'

'Okay. I'll tame the lions, and you can walk the high wire dressed like a ballerina.'

'Promise?' I said, as I finished my sandwich.

'On my honor,' he said, and gave me a quick kiss on the cheek. 'It'll be you and me to the end of the line.'

Robby shifted in his chair and gave me

the evil eye. 'I think you should drink your milk now,' he said.

I slid off Rafe's lap and drank my milk halfway down, but it didn't mixed very well with the beer. I didn't feel so chipper anymore.

Robby grabbed my hand and rushed me to the bathroom. My stomach lurched. I folded over the toilet and upchucked.

'Just in time,' I said, with a goofy grin. The room spun around me and I couldn't get back up.

I heard the screen door shut as Rafe walked back toward the barn.

Robby pulled me to my feet and I leaned against his arm.

'I don't want you talking to Rafe unless there's someone else around,' said Robby. 'It's not like we know a damn thing about the guy.'

'You're not my dad. You can't tell me what to do.'

The green feeling swept over me again. I turned back to the toilet and threw up what little was left in my stomach.

While Robby cleaned up all traces of our noontime bacchanal, I lay on my bed, too dizzy to move. I was still a bit tipsy when Dad and Bell returned from Gunnar.

I threw my arms around Dad's waist. 'What did the doctor say? Are you going to be okay?'

'They ran more tests. I'll know more in a day or two,' he said, as Robby and I helped him to his room. 'The doctor thinks I might have a virus.'

'You kids come to the table,' called Bell, after we'd spent about twenty minutes keeping Dad company. 'Leave your dad alone. You're only tiring him out.'

Rafe sauntered in from outdoors and we all took our places at the table. Bell opened the fridge.

'Who's been into the roast beef?' she said. 'And the milk is almost gone!'

'It was me,' I said, feeling uncharacteristically fearless in the aftermath of all that beer. 'I think I'm having a growth spurt.'

'A growth spurt? Sounds more like a tapeworm, if you ask me.'

I glanced at Rafe, who looked at me with a big grin on his face. I started to giggle, and pretty soon Robby couldn't keep a straight face either.

'I don't see what's so funny,' said Bell, which made us laugh all the harder.

During dinner, Bell gave me an icy look. My beer bravado had worn off. I knew she'd retaliate. She wasn't the kind of person who let things go.

For the next couple days I hung out by Dad's bedside or stayed close to Robby as he did his chores. Then one quiet afternoon when I thought Bell was gathering eggs she caught me foraging in the forbidden pantry. She grabbed me and shook me like a rag doll.

'I'm hungry. The peanut butter is gone. I want some lentil soup.'

'You know that soup is for your father's recovery.'

Recovery? That wasn't what I'd call it.

Bell was wearing another dowdy cotton dress with a faded floursack apron, her hair pulled back in a tight bun like an old-maid schoolteacher, a pair of shlumpy brogues on her feet.

'Why don't you leave?' I said. 'We were happy before you came.'

I'd struck a nerve. I covered my head

and let my arms take the brunt of the blows.

'You make me gag!' I shrieked.

'What's going on in there?' called Dad from his sickbed.

Bell clamped a hand over my mouth.

'Abby saw a rat in the pantry, but it's all taken care of, Edward.'

'I certainly hope so,' he said, in a voice that had become weak and whispery.

'I'll bring you some lunch in just a minute.'

Bell turned to me. 'You utter a single word against me and it's the last one you'll ever do,' she said, removing her hand from my mouth.

As I fled the pantry I tripped over a big jug of greenish-yellow liquid that stuck out from beneath the bottom shelf. I regained my footing and kept going, but I didn't forget about the jug.

As I bolted out the back door I heard Bell calling Sheba, reminding me of her threat to cook her in the microwave. Sheba and Kelly were long out of harm's way, but I now found myself at the top of Bell's hit list.

Late that night Robby and I smuggled the jug of green stuff into the tractor shed. Robby turned on his flashlight and saw the bruises on my arms.

'Geez, Abby, what happened?'

'What do you think? Shine the light on the label.'

'I don't have to,' said Robby. 'It's ethylene glycol. Everybody calls it anti-freeze. Dad keeps a jug in the garage to keep the car from freezing up in winter. It's poison, and hard to detect on a blood test unless you're specifically looking for it. Antifreeze poisoning mimics a lot of other ailments.'

'How do you know so much?'

'It came up for discussion in science class. What if Bell is putting it in Dad's soup? Do you ever remember him being sick before she came along?'

'Nothing worse than a cold. What are we going to do?'

'For now we can hide it. It will give us time to plan out next step.'

We walked across the damp grass in our pajamas and hid the jug in the long-abandoned outhouse.

The next morning Dad had a seizure at the breakfast table. It was very scary. I started to cry as his cup rattled in the saucer and fell to the floor. Robby ran to the phone and called Dr. McBane, who told us to meet him at the ER.

Bell grabbed the phone out of Robby's hand and slammed it into the cradle.

'From now on, stay off the telephone unless you have my express permission to use it. I don't want to have to remind you again who's in charge here.'

'I'll help you get Dad to the car,' said Robby. 'I want to talk to Dr. McBane. I want to know what's going on with Dad.'

'Are you sick?' asked Bell.

'I didn't say I was sick. Neither was Dad until a few weeks ago.'

Dad's tremors subsided. He looked at Robby like he wanted to say something, but the words wouldn't come. For the first time there was fear in his kind blue eyes. He tensed when Bell touched him, and she knew that we knew.

Bell turned her attention to Robby. 'While we're gone I want you and Abby to chop a box of kindling. Come on, Rafe.

Help me get him to the car.'

I leaned close to Dad's ear as he was loaded into the back seat. 'I love you, Dad.'

* * *

Hell with the kindling. As soon as the car was out of sight, Robby and I went back to the attic.

'We need those phony documents to make our case. We need to get them to the sheriff.'

The suitcase wasn't where we'd left it. We pawed deep into the corners of the attic behind trunks and boxes and old bedframes. We tried Bell's bedroom door but it was locked.

'Hey, babe. Whatch lookin' for?'

I nearly jumped out of my skin. It was Robby, throwing his voice like he had when Jimbo was still around. I punched him on the shoulder.

'You scared me shitless!' I said, still shaking. 'You sounded just like Rafe.'

'I've been practicing behind the barn.'

'Well, don't practice on me.'

We spent another half hour searching the house and came up empty. The suitcase could be anywhere — the hayloft, under the floorboards, or in the rafters of the garage. She could have separated the items and hidden them in various places. For now it was a lost cause. Bell knew we were on to her, and she was on to us.

'Let's call the ER,' said Robby. 'Let's see what we can find out on our own.' We ran downstairs and Robby dialed the phone in the kitchen.

'Emergency Room. Nurse Lindsey speaking. How may I help you?'

'This is Robby Granger, ma'am. I'd like to speak with Dr. McBane. He's our family physician and I believe he's with my father, Edward.'

'Let me check.' Within a minute she'd returned. 'The doctor is busy, but I can put Mrs. Granger on the phone.'

'No, that's okay. She can fill me in when she gets home.'

He quickly hung up the phone.

When Dad returned our hopes for his recovery dimmed.

'Why wasn't he admitted?' I asked.

'I convinced the doctor to wait a day or two and see how the new medication works. Hospital stays can run into the thousands of dollars.'

'You mean his life isn't worth the expense?' I said.

'You watch your tongue.'

'Have they run a toxicology test?' asked Robby.

'Oh my, aren't we using big words these days?' said Bell. 'You take one science class and you think you're Lawrence Pasteur.'

'I've had two advanced classes, and it's Louis — not Lawrence.'

If her grey eyes were bullets, there would have been two holes in his chest.

Suddenly, Dad spoke for the first time in days. He was staring at my arms.

'Where — all — bruises?' he said, faintly.

'I'm not sure. Maybe Bell remembers.'

Did he understand what I was trying to say? I couldn't tell.

Bell glared at me. 'You're simply a clumsy kid. I told you to be more careful.'

After I crawled into bed that night I heard Bell climb the stairs to my room. I cringed inwardly as she sat on the edge of my mattress.

'Have you been talking with Pastor Blevins about our family business?' she asked. 'Or anyone else, for that matter? Some things aren't to be discussed outside the family circle.'

'What's to talk about?'

'I want you to stay out of your father's room. He needs his rest, and conversing takes too much out of him. Doctor's orders.' She leaned closer. 'You like it here on the farm, don't you?'

'Yes. I was born here.'

'Farms are nice places to grow up, but they're dangerous places, Abby, even for smart little girls who think they know it all. Kids get kicked by horses. They fall down wells. They stumble into empty silos. Sometimes they vanish without explanation and their bones are never found. It would be a shame if something like that happened to a curious little girl like you.'

That night I dreamt that Dad, Robby and I lay at the bottom of a deep, dark well. Fifty feet above us, Bell was smiling and looking over the circular rim. I woke in the morning with fever and chills and a storm raging overhead.

The power went out with a spray of sparks along the wires between the highway and the house.

When Bell decided to go into town to fill Dad's prescriptions, we piled into his room. Having us near him gave him the energy to sit up in bed, so Robby decided to put on a show. I sat in a chair beside Dad's bed while Robby went through his repertoire of voices. He did Auntie Pearl's dry cackle, Pastor Blevin's basso profundo, Cousin Ralphy's adenoidal wheeze, and Rafe's sexy baritone. By the time he took his final bow, the color had risen in Dad's cheeks and a bit of the old spark had returned to his eyes.

'You kids are good medicine,' he said. 'I'm feeling better than I have for a while.'

A draft blew under the door and seeped in around the window frames. 'It must be terribly cold in the tack room,' said Dad. 'Why don't you invite Rafe to come in and warm up? Tell him there's coffee in the kitchen.'

Before Robby could move, I jumped up and flew past him, dashing into the rain, splashing through the puddles. By the time I reached the barn, rain was dripping from my pigtails, the ribbons limp and bedraggled.

The barn was shadowy and smelled of sweet alfalfa and fresh straw. Rafe kept everything shipshape: cows milked, stalls clean, garden weeded. I didn't think we could have managed without him since Dad got sick.

It might have been a sound beneath the clatter of the rain, or just a funny feeling that tickled along my spine, but for whatever reason, I stopped short of the tack room where Rafe had his cot. The door was open but I still held back. I heard voices and ducked into an empty stall across the aisle. Rafe and Bell were talking. She hadn't left for town after all. I was curious. I wondered what they talked about when the rest of us weren't around.

'The doctors don't suspect a thing,' she said. 'I'm just a loving wife concerned about my husband's deteriorating health, but it's the kids could queer the whole deal. They're not the dumb little bumpkins I thought they'd be.' A rumble of thunder rolled across the sky. I missed the next part of the conversation, but I didn't miss what followed.

Rafe ran his hand up Bell's thigh. She laughed and threw her head back. Until now I'd never seen her so much as smile. He pulled her close and kissed her throat. She didn't bolt. She didn't slap his face. In one fluid movement she unbuttoned her shabby cotton dress and let it drop around her ankles. Everything she wore under it was next to go. Her pale body rippled with rain shadows. To my astonishment she had long shapely legs, a slender waist and youthful breasts. Her drab exterior had been concealing a centerfold body. She was like an actress pulling off a quick change between scenes. I was stunned, my feet frozen to the floor.

Rafe pulled the hairpins from Bell's tightly coiled bun. An ocean of light brown waves burst free and fell halfway down her back. The old Bell vanished. Who the hell was this new creature? Rafe kicked off his boots and stepped out of his jeans. I'd heard people say *naked as a jaybird* before, but I'd never seen a bird that looked quite like this. When they folded downward into the straw, I ran.

My heart thundered. I could barely breathe. I raced from the barn, confused and afraid. Bell was no longer Bell, and Rafe had broken my heart. There never would be a circus. *Together forever* was a big fat lie.

I flew into the house and ran up the stairs past Robby. I sat in the corner of the attic and cried. Robbie came through the door and locked it behind him.

'What happened to you?' he said, sitting on the floor beside me. 'Did Rafe hurt you? Tell me the truth.'

'It was something else,' I said. 'Bell hadn't left for town yet like Dad thought. I caught them in the barn doing something.'

'Who?'

'Bell and Rafe.'

'Like what?'

I was only ten. I didn't have the right words, but I tried my best. 'They were all twisted up in the hay without their clothes on. She didn't look at all like the everyday Bell. She's putting on a pious act, but she's someone else entirely.'

Robby wiped my tears with his t-shirt

'You're safe now. You don't have to be afraid. I'd stay away from them both as much as you can.'

'Rafe and I were going to join the circus.'

'You can't always count on people doing what they say, Abby.'

'I thought he loved me.'

'I know.'

For a few minutes we sat listening to the rain

'There's either something *really* weird going on here, or they aren't sister and brother like they say,' said Robby. 'I don't see a family resemblance, do you?'

'No. Nothing I can think of.'

'On the other hand, they're not exactly strangers.'

'If they were, they aren't anymore,' I said.

We shared a moment of quiet laughter and I started feeling a little better. By the time we came down from the attic we'd formulated a plan.

The rain was over by dinnertime and the power had been restored. When Bell returned home with Dad's prescriptions she warmed his soup and poured it into a bowl.

'I think that soup should be tested,' I blurted out. 'It could be swimming with salmonella or botulism. It's been sitting around too long.'

'If it was going to make him better, he wouldn't still be sick,' said Robby.

A quick glance passed between Bell and Rafe. On her way to the table she tripped on a tear in the linoleum and spilled the soup on the floor.

'Now look at what you made me do,' she said.

I volunteered to clean up the mess.

I couldn't say it wasn't weird eating meatloaf and mashed potatoes like a *Leave It to Beaver* family, knowing what I'd witnessed that afternoon. Bell had slipped effortlessly back into her drab persona, Rafe ignoring her like she didn't exist.

That evening I slipped enough Benedryl into Dad's hot chocolate to keep him under until the cock crowed.

At midnight, when everyone was asleep, Robby and I coasted the John Deere mower down the driveway, fired it up at the road and drove the empty mile to the convenience store. Once inside the outdoor phone booth, Robby dialed home. After a few rings Bell picked up.

'I gotta see you, baby,' he said, in Rafe's sexy rumble. 'I'm at Mike's Bar. Wear that sexy red job. Let's be us, even if it's only for one night.'

Robby hung up before she could respond.

'What if she checks the tack room first?'

'Then we're screwed, but I doubt she will. She's dying to let her hair down.'

When we got back the pickup was gone and Dad was still heavily sedated. I ran to the tack room and woke Rafe. Despite everything I knew, some bit of my heart still belonged to him, but I knew what I had to do. I handed him the keys to Dad's old Ford.

'Bell called, all upset. She needs you at Mike's Bar — something about engine trouble.'

'What's she doing alone at Mike's?' I

saw the flicker of jealousy in his eyes and I knew he'd go.

The moment he pulled onto the highway, we called Pastor Blevins. Halfway through our story he was out of bed and dressed.

'I'm calling an ambulance for your dad,' he said. 'Then I'm coming to get you two in case Bell and Rafe get suspicious and return unexpectedly. I'm in the mood for a little rabble-rousing in the name of the Lord.'

Both of the Granger vehicles were parked outside Mike's Bar when we walked through the swinging doors. It was a rowdy place, as evidenced by the baseball bat at Mike's elbow. Hank Williams was warbling 'Your Cheating Heart' from the juke box. I was ten years old and no one had to tell me about cheating hearts or broken ones. I knew all there was to know, or thought I did at the time.

There was a No Smoking sign above the bar, but the cigarette smoke was so thick you could hardly see your hand in front of your face. My eyes watered and I coughed a couple times. Pastor Blevins pressed me against the wall in the small space between the jukebox and a tall wooden Indian.

'Don't move until I come get you,' he said.

Rafe sat at the bar in his plaid shirt and jeans, and my heart broke all over again. Beside him sat Bell, smoking a Virginia Slim in a black cigarette holder. She wore the blonde wig we'd seen in the suitcase, the red dress and stiletto shoes. Her eyes were made up Egyptian-style, her lips painted fire-engine red. No one in the room, man or woman, could keep their eyes off of her, either catching her image in the big mirror behind the bar or just staring as if she were an exotic animal on display.

'Bell Jones!' boomed Pastor Blevins, over the ambient roar. The room fell silent. Men laid down their pool cues. There was a flicker of fear in her eyes as she looked at the pastor. Every eye in the room was watching her. She tossed back the rest of her drink and slid from the stool.

'Let's get out of here, Rafe.' She turned

to the crowd. 'It's just that crazy minister who's been stalking me,' she said. Everyone in town knew Pastor Blevins. No one believed a word she said. As she moved toward the door, Rafe followed. There was no question as to who ran the show.

'Call Sheriff Gunderson,' said Pastor Blevins, addressing Mike.

Mike picked up the phone. 'He might not be that easy to find on a Saturday night.'

'Well, try. There are two people here who are up to no good, and I want the sheriff to run a background check on both of them.'

Bell tried to push past the preacher, but he blocked the exit. I sneezed from the smoke in the room and she whipped her head in my direction.

'You little brat! You're behind this,' she screeched. Her eyes were wild as she lifted her satin skirt and pulled the muff gun out of her garter. She aimed at my head. Robby jumped in front of me, and Rafe spun Bell toward him and grabbed the barrel of the gun. She shoved the business end of the gun to his chest and pulled the trigger. A man in a cowboy hat quickly disarmed her, and held her before she could get off the second bullet, but it seemed that one was all that was needed. Rafe lay on the floor amid the spilled beer and cigarette butts, fighting for air.

'Call 911,' said Blevins. 'We need an ambulance. Tell them to hurry.'

I pushed past Robby and knelt beside Rafe. His face was very pale.

'I can't seem to catch my breath, Abby.'

A man came over and helped me unbutton his shirt.

'You're going to be fine, Rafe. It's only a tiny little hole,' I said. He tried to lift his hand. I took it and held it tight.

'I haven't forgotten my promise, Abby. In a few years we'll be off to the circus, you and me.'

'And you won't let me down?

I wanted so desperately to believe him that for a moment I allowed his words to be true.

'Would I lie to you, Princess?'

His grip on my hand loosened and he was gone.

'Where the hell is that ambulance?'

boomed Pastor Blevins.

Mike hung up the phone. 'Gunnar only has one, and it's just now leaving the Granger farm with Ed.'

'You can forget the ambulance,' said the man who'd helped me with the shirt. 'This man needs a coroner.'

I stood up and walked over to where the cowboy had Bell's arms pinned behind her back.

'You were my one mistake, Abby,' she said. 'I should have done you in first.'

'I guess you should have,' I said. 'Where do you come from? Who is the real you?'

Bell snorted a cynical laugh. 'Hell, kid. I've used so many aliases in so many towns, I'll be damned if I have a clue.'

* * *

That was years ago now. Dad recovered and walked me down the aisle when I married the oldest son from the Hayden farm. Robby married my husband's younger sister. There's not a large pool of marital candidates in a place like Gunnar, but all it takes is one good one.

Bell died in Federal prison somewhere in Nebraska. I seldom think about her, but I do think about Rafe — my first serious case of puppy love — whenever the circus passes through town. I believe to this day there was good in the man, that he had some genuine feeling for me. If that were not true, the bullet meant for me would not be lodged in his heart.

Bullet for a Boxer

As I crossed the alley between the pawn shop and the Rescue Mission, a bullet slammed into my head and dropped me to my knees. It felt like a brick falling from a building, but there was no mistaking the telltale pop and the lingering smell of cordite. My hand flew to the long rip where the bullet had surfed across my scalp. I struggled to retain consciousness as blood dripped between my fingers.

It was too dark to see the shooter, but I heard the rapid retreat of shoes slapping against the wet concrete, followed by a car squealing down the access alley behind the buildings on the main drag. It was a moment before I was convinced the bullet had not penetrated the quivering jelly of my brain. I guessed this was my lucky night, if you want to look at it that way. The bullet was probably lodged in the wall of the pawn shop, but at the moment I was more concerned with reaching the safety of my flat above the bar than I was with collecting evidence.

Standing at the bathroom sink I finally stemmed the bleeding. I clipped away the thinning hair around the wound, then closed it as best I could with Band-Aids. Tonight's schedule was already full with no openings for doctors and cops and lengthy interrogations.

I collapsed in my easy chair by the window overlooking Cork Street. Loops of neon light from the closed businesses across the street flickered through the rain. I downed a restorative shot of brandy and tapped a Lucky Strike from the pack. With an unsteady hand I lighted the tip with a silver Ronson that had outlasted my boxing career, my liver and Laura — beautiful Laura. Her smiling face met my gaze from a framed photo on the bookcase across the room.

Of course, there had been others since my wife walked out those many years ago, bleached blondes and redheads in war-paint who whispered little lies in my ear and saved the whoppers for their husbands. They meant about as much to me as I did to them — a tonic to wash away the isolation of the lonely and left behind. That's the way it is when you're still in love with a ghost.

I took a long drag from my cigarette and pulled the smoke deep into my center. I held it a moment, then exhaled toward the ceiling. Who would waste a bullet on a washed-up boxer? I'd like to think it was a careless misfire, but the knot in my gut told me otherwise.

'Michael, the musicians are here.'

That would be Tully calling up the staircase. He'd been pulling the spigots at the Cork Street Bar and Grill long before my dad passed the business on to me. I could hear the instruments tuning up for the St. Patrick's Day celebration. Tonight was booked. Tomorrow I'd rest.

I reached for the doorknob and there were two of them. I felt around until I found the real one. I'd been in the boxing game long enough to know my brain was swelling like bread dough, but I hadn't missed the St. Patrick's Day celebration since I was a kid. I was expected to make a showing. I popped a green bowler on my head and descended the stairs to the bar.

I survived half an hour of drums, fiddles and the Irish whistle, but when Ben Feeley began torturing the bagpipes, my head spun like the Irish dancers at the front of the room. I understood with sudden clarity why the English had banned the bagpipes as a weapon of war. The noise was certainly killing me.

'You're looking a bit green around the gills, me boyo,' said Tully, tufts of white hair poking from under his derby. 'What you need is a nice foamy mug of green beer. Last chance until next St. Pat's Day.'

My stomach lurched.

'I think I'll lie down. A touch of the flu,' I said. 'Doyle can back you up. He can always use the hours.'

The moment my head hit the pillow the room began to spin. I lit a Lucky, but it dropped into the folds of the blanket. I was scrambling to find it when my stomach cartwheeled and I staggered toward the bathroom. Things would have worked out fine if the bathroom had been where I'd left it just this morning. My feet tangled, my shoulder hit the wall and I stumbled to my knees. When I looked down there was a big black hole where the floor had been. I slid toward the edge, grabbed a handful of air and tumbled downward.

⋆ ⋆ ⋆

When I hit the bottom it was 1934 again. I knew because I recognized the poster tacked to the wall. It promoted tonight's heavyweight bout between me, Michael 'The Mick' Gannon, and Vito 'The Wop' Antonelli.

My trainer, Jinx Riley, an energetic little leprechaun with a wild thicket of eyebrows, was taping my hands and lacing me into my gloves. He warned me once more about Vito's mean left hook, to keep my head tucked into my right shoulder and my wits about me. Yeah, yeah, yeah! I was a cocky twenty-year-old, too stupid to know I didn't have all the answers. You couldn't tell me a damn thing.

My manager, Jerry Featherstone leaned against the wall in his London-tailored suit, his stylish fedora at a rakish tilt. I was the one got knocked around out there. It was my blood on the mat, so how come it was Jerry scored the five-course dinners and I got fish and chips? In this racket you either turn a blind eye to the mysteries of backroom bookkeeping or stand in the breadline.

Last year I'd been climbing the ladder toward a match with Ernie Schaaf, but when Primo Camera knocked him out in the ring, Ernie never came out of his coma and died hours later. Scrambling for another match to fill the void, Jerry arranged a bout with up-and-comer, Vito Antonelli. Tonight we both go into the ring undefeated. By the end of the night, one of our records will fall.

As Jinx finished tightening the laces of my gloves, Laura watched me quietly from across the room. Her dark hair cascaded over the shoulders of her white suit; long, shapely legs shimmering in silk stockings. You'd never know from looking at her that she was three months pregnant.

She walked across the room and gave me a lingering hug. I breathed in the scent of her floral perfume. She lived in a constant state of anxiety over my choice of career. What if something happened to me? What would become of her? How would she raise a baby by herself at the height of the Great Depression? But hell, all I had was the fight racket since Prohibition closed my dad's bar. She knew who I was and what I did when she married me. In those days I saw one side of every issue. Mine.

The first time I met Laura, she was performing with an Irish dance troupe at my dad's bar. She was sixteen and the prettiest girl I'd ever seen. I turned to Dad and said, *Laura Kelly has eyes bluer than the sapphires in the jeweler's window.* Of course, I should have kept my thoughts to myself, because Dad looked at Tully and Tully looked at Dad and they laughed their asses off at my expense. *The lad's got it bad,* they agreed. Two years later I had the last laugh when Laura and I walked down the aisle of St. Finnbar's Church.

I kissed Laura on the cheek and told her not to worry, then handed her a dime to get me a pack of smokes from the machine down the hall. I needed a few seconds alone with Jerry.

'I want you to send her home in a cab before the fight starts,' I said. 'She's not cut out for this.'

'She's not cut out to be a fighter's wife,' said Jerry.

'Shut your gob,' I said. 'I didn't hire you to give advice on my personal life. Just send her home before the opening bell.'

The crowd began to roar and stomp their feet. The entire auditorium vibrated.

'Showtime,' said Jinx.

* * *

There was a buzzing in my ears. Someone was slapping my face and calling my name. I didn't remember the round I went down in, but I had to be on my feet by the count of ten.

'Michael, it's Dr. Weinburg. Open your eyes for me.'

I opened them halfway, but the light hurt my head. I saw Tully in a chair across the room and wondered where Jerry and Jinx had gone.

'Was it the left hook?' I asked the doctor.

'There was no fight,' he said. 'This is nineteen-fifty, Michael. When Mrs. Grady came to do the cleaning yesterday, she found you on the floor, a hole burned in your blankets and a bullet lodged beneath your scalp.'

'I thought it went into the pawn shop wall,' I said.

I reached up and felt the zipper of stitches on my crown. Dr. Weinburg leaned over the bed and checked my pupils with a thin but intense beam of light.

'Still mismatched,' he said to Tully. 'Michael, can you think of anyone who's out to get you?'

'Then or now?' I asked.

'Now would be more relevant,' he said patiently.

'The lad's still not with us,' said Tully. 'He's back in his boxing days.'

'You have a concussion,' said Weinburg. 'We're going to keep you in another day or two.' He held something up between his fingers. 'Do you know what this is?'

'It's a bullet, Doc.'

'I found it between your scalp and your skull. You're lucky you've got a thick one or your yolk would be leaking out of the shell. Do you have an explanation for the event that brought you here?'

'Not really. Does it mean I lost the bout?'

* * *

A few days later I was almost myself again. Lieutenant Frank Cullen came to the hospital to get my statement, the bullet being placed in his custody. Frank and I had gone to school together and maintained our friendship through the years.

'You got a beef with anyone in particular?' he asked. 'Maybe a disgruntled customer down at the Cork?'

'Just Father Kilgore. He said I should be crucified, but he never said anything about a gun.'

'And this would be in relation to what?'

'I told him to take his business down

the road, that we got no use for priests with a penchant for altar boys.'

'Hmm!' he said. 'Anybody else on the shortlist? Any gambling debts or husbands out for blood?'

'Not recently.'

* * *

In my absence Mrs. Grady had cleaned my room and thrown out my burned bedding. She made me swear on her dead husband's rosary not to smoke in bed. So as not to disappoint her, I waited until she was gone before I sank back on the clean white pillows and lit up. Women may come and go over the years. The same is true of fame and boxing titles. But even if you're sick, broke and down on your luck, there's always the cigarettes to keep you from tumbling into the void.

Around seven that night Tully brought me a corned beef on rye and a pint of Guinness to wash down the sleeping pills. When I was done I drifted off to the tap of rain on the window, thinking about the days when my dad was the king of Cork

Street and ran numbers out of the back room. Between the drugs and a lingering fever, I dreamt in color like when I was a kid.

Sometime after midnight the wind came up and rain came down in blustery swirls. The phone rang beside my bed and I grappled, half-comatose, for the receiver. 'The bar is closed,' I mumbled. A branch of lightning flickered on the horizon and sparks shot from an electrical wire on the pole outside my window.

'I know it is.' A woman's voice. Sad. Misty. Vaguely familiar.

I tried to shake off the effects of the sleeping pills. A draft leaked under the door as the wind sent a quiver through the bones of the old building. I smelled a faint hint of perfume.

'Is that you?' I said.

'I've missed you all these years.'

'I'm dreaming,' I said, wrapped in brain fog.

'I know, Michael, but you didn't dream the bullet.' In her voice was a bit of the Irish cadence. If you're raised in the Cork neighborhood, you could live twenty years in China and never get rid of the Irish music on your tongue.

'Look behind you, Michael. Way back. Your life has become an unwelcome chapter in someone else's book.'

'What does that mean?'

'Just something to think about.'

The transformer outside my window exploded like a bomb and the phone went dead.

'Laura?' I said. 'Laura, is that you?'

There was no reply.

When I woke the next morning the receiver was lying on the floor beside my bed.

* * *

I came downstairs to find Tully working the grill. An elderly couple were playing checkers at a corner table and three men who worked the day shift at the meat-packing house were tossing back an eye-opener with mountains of fried potatoes.

'Well, look at you all showered and shaved,' said Tully. 'You up for some breakfast?'

'Sure. How about a cup of black coffee and a Bloody Mary?'

'Coming right up.'

After the early crowd thinned out, Tully took a stool next to mine. He poured a shot of Scotch into his coffee and lit a cigarette. 'So, what's up? You sure you're supposed to be out of bed?'

I squeezed the lemon wedge in my drink and set it on the paper napkin.

'Have you kept in touch with any of the old crowd?' I asked

'You mean from the fight days?' I nodded. 'Not since you bowed out. You did the right thing. Boxing isn't a train you can ride into your golden years. Be thankful you left with all your marbles. A lot of boys left 'em on the mat.'

I added a squirt of Worcestershire to my drink.

'Laura's been on my mind lately,' I said, without mentioning the dream.

'Why now? She's been gone since the late thirties. Drunk driver took her out head-on.'

'In San Jose, right? Don't you find it odd that in the years before she died, she never filed for divorce?'

'Yeah, I do. My exes couldn't wait to drag me in front of the judge. There's been a lot of water gone under the bridge since those days.' He took a long pull from his cigarette. 'You know, there is a name that comes up now and then. Vito. He's doing a stretch for second-degree murder.'

'No shit!' I said. 'Why am I not surprised?'

* * *

Antonelli and I sat on opposite sides of the glass partition with in-house receivers pressed to our ears. Since we'd last come face to face, my red hair had faded and thinned and Vito had become shrunken and stooped, his neck and arms black with prison tats. He proudly showed off the ink on his left arm.

''Born To Lose'?' I said. 'I admire a man who can predict his destiny with such clarity.'

'But I didn't lose that night, did I?'

'You got me there,' I conceded. 'Put me

in a two-week coma. When I came out of it, the world I remembered wasn't there anymore.'

He smiled, his teeth brown with cigarette stains, one incisor missing. 'You mean Laura,' he said. 'You'd have lost her anyway. I heard she miscarried the night of the fight all because you made her sit ringside and watch the bloodbath.'

'That's a —lie!' I almost lunged at the glass partition and Vito instinctively jerked back in his seat. The guard looked over and I lowered my voice. 'Who told you that?'

He crossed his arms over his chest. 'Who cares? It's ancient history. All I know is Jinx moved on to train that Jew flyweight who took the title, and Jerry left for parts unknown. As for Laura . . . Poof! Up in smoke. No one heard anything until the crash. You want to know more than that, you'll have to get a crystal ball.'

I took a deep breath and pulled back from the glass.

'I lost my focus that night. Jinx told me to watch your left hook.'

If a rat could laugh, he'd look like Vito.

'It wasn't my left hook that cancelled your ticket, you chump. It was the eight-ounce lead sinker in my glove.' He leaned forward in his seat. 'It sure as hell sank your ship.'

It all came back in a sickening rush — the knockout, the blood on my brain, the busted jaw, shattered right eye socket and crushed cheekbone. I felt the color drain from my skin like I was back there, living it all over again.

'What, you couldn't take me like a man?' I said. 'Maybe that's why I'm out here and you're in there.'

'Listen up. I wasn't there to take you. I had orders to kill you, to take you out permanent, you dumb Mick.'

I sat in stunned silence.

'Are you telling me the Ganguzzas were behind this?' I said, referring to the head of the local mob back then. 'Even with me out of the picture you never got a shot at Camera, so what good did it do?'

'You ain't listening. That's the trouble with you potato-heads. The order wasn't coming from my end.' He looked steadily into my eyes until the message sank in. I guess it was the head injury made me a little slow.

'You can't mean *my* camp? Who are we talking about here?'

'My trainer was too smart — or too scared — to let me in on that. It was on a need-to-know basis and I was out of the loop. I just wanted the money. It was the Great Depression. I had a wife and three kids, for Chrissake. They told me I did half a job, so I got half the pay and that was it.'

'Come on, Vito. You spaghetti-jockeys always know more than you let on.'

'We know when to keep our mouths shut. That's why I'm still alive. Why don't you ask Jinx Riley?'

'Jinx? I didn't know he was still around.'

'Word is, he won't be for long. Uncle Vin tells me he's in a care facility outside Stockton. He's hooked up to one of them machines with all the tubes and whistles.'

'You know so much, maybe you know who tried to blow my head off last week.' I lifted my cap so he could get a good look at Weinburg's handiwork. He found the situation amusing and gave a rat-laugh.

'You are one unlucky SOB.'

* * *

Driving back to Santa Paulina, the late-afternoon sun piercing my eyes, my head began hammering. My liver was slightly distended below my right ribcage, and I made another half-hearted resolution to cut back on the booze. I couldn't keep my mind on the road. At a rural intersection I slammed into a skid and nearly rear-ended a truck carrying crates of live turkeys. The driver, shaking from head to toe, jumped out of the cab and dressed me down in broken English. I didn't understand a word but I got the message.

It was dusk when I pulled into the back parking lot. I looked around for any gun-toting bad guys lurking in the shadows and, seeing nothing but a stray cat raiding the garbage can, walked up the back staircase to my flat. Frank Cullen had left his star-embellished card stuck in the crack of the door with his home phone scribbled on the back.

I switched on the light and dropped Frank's card on the end table, feeling almost as bad as I had in the hospital — headache — blurry vision — cold sweat popping out on my forehead. I headed straight to the bathroom and washed down a handful of various pills with a swig of mouthwash, then dropped my dead weight on the bed and slept in my clothes.

The next morning I felt almost human. I ate a real breakfast at the bar, washed it down with three cups of coffee and skipped the Bloody Mary. I turned to Tully, who was scraping the grill with something that sounded like fingernails on a blackboard.

'You want to take a drive?' I asked. 'I almost cracked up the car yesterday.'

He stopped scraping and turned around. 'Sure, I can drive. What about the bar?'

'Call Doyle. He'll be here before you can hang up the phone.'

* * *

Tully decided to remain in the waiting room while I walked to Room A-12. The place smelled like faded flowers and rubbing alcohol. Jinx scarcely made a ripple beneath the covers, machines clicking and beeping at bedside. I touched the back of his hand. It was thin and cold, his lips a cyanotic blue.

'Jinx,' I said. He opened his eyes. The bright blue irises I remembered so vividly were clouded with cataracts.

'Well, I'll be damned if it isn't Mike 'The Mick' Gannon,' he said, his voice as thin and dry as paper. 'What the hell happened to you? I thought you were your old man.' He chuckled softly.

'I guess time caught up with me.' I smiled and sat in a chair at the bedside. I patted the back of his hand. 'Looks like you're not doing so well, partner.'

'The doc blames it on cigarettes. I'd have one now if it weren't for all these damn tubes. God, it's good to see one of the old crowd. You could punch a hole in a brick wall with that right of yours.'

'Those were the days.'

'You bet they were. When I was a kid,

us Micks owned the fight game, whole neighborhoods of young boys pouring into the gym. Then came the Jews — some damn good fighters there; and the Italians — and could their moms ever cook! We didn't know what cooking was before they moved into the neighborhood. At home it was a stubborn piece of meat keeping company with a boiled potato. The Irish know how to drink, but nobody ever taught 'em how to cook.'

'Growing up in the Cork was quite a circus.'

'Boxing was going to make us all rich, buy our moms fancy hats and houses on the right side of the tracks. It came true for a few of us.'

I loved Jinx. He was a talker. Hell, all of us Corkys were. Put us six feet under, we'd go down talking. As I sat by his bedside we revisited all the great fights, the betting and the fixes and the guys who died in the ring. When we got to the Gannon-Antonelli bout, I told him about my conversation with Vito.

'That kid was a rotten apple,' said Jinx. 'He's where he belongs.'

'You think he was bullshitting me, or was there a bowling ball in his glove like he says?'

'I always felt that win was bogus. Yes, he was good, but not that good. The velocity of that punch would have rocked you, maybe even decked you; but without a loaded glove, you'd have been back on your feet.'

'He said the fix came from our end. Do you believe that, or is he full of hot air?'

A flame jumped in Jinx's eyes and a bit of the old fight returned.

'That's horsepucky, boy. Doesn't make sense. You were our ticket to the big time. It had to be the Italians, the Ganguzzas or Zanferdinos. They always bet big on Antonelli.'

'Consider this. A TKO would have gotten them their money, but Vito said someone wanted me dead. The Italians had no motive to kill me. No one wants their boxer killing his opponent in the ring. It's something the public never gets out of their head.'

'Now that I think of it, you may be right . . . but if not them, who?'

Jinx grabbed my hand. He was having trouble breathing. I rose from the chair and leaned over the bed. The oxygen tubes had slipped out of his nose and I readjusted them.

'You want the nurse?' I said.

'Thanks. I'm okay now.'

I didn't realize I'd lost my cap when I bent over the bed, and that Jinx had noticed the fancy stitchery on my scalp.

'What happened?' he said, as I slipped my hat back on. 'One of your patrons get out of hand?'

'Some things never change,' I said, and left it at that.

'Ain't it the truth.' His laughter ended in coughing and he spat blood into a napkin. He finally caught his breath and a little color came back into his face. If it wasn't the Italians crossed me up, it had to be Jinx or Jerry, and I didn't want to go there.

The lunch cart rolled down the hall, and we said our goodbyes.

As Tully and I headed toward the exit door, a nurse trotted over and handed me a cardboard box.

'Mr. Riley wants you to have this,' she said. 'It's his boxing scrapbook and fight memorabilia, the sum of his worldly possessions. I'm glad you came, gentlemen. He doesn't get many visitors.'

'Please thank him. Tell him I'll be back next week.'

'Mr. Gannon, we'll be lucky if he makes it through the night.'

* * *

When we got back to the bar, Tully went home to get some shut-eye. Lieutenant Cullen was sitting at the bar eating a hamburger with fries. I remembered with a jolt that I'd forgotten to get back to him.

'Bring the officer another beer, Doyle, and tear up his check while you're at it. He's an old friend of the family.'

'You're a corrupting influence just like your old man was,' said Frank as we carried our beers to a back booth. 'Did you see my card?' he added as we got settled.

'I had to go out of town. What's up?'

'Since the incident I've been keeping

an eye on you. You and Tully picked up a tail on your way out of town this morning — a guy in a black Buick, the same guy I saw parked across from the bar yesterday.'

'Did you ID him?'

'I followed him for a few miles, then pulled him over. His name is Paul Ratner.'

'Never heard of him.'

'Tall. Bony. Face like a death mask.'

I couldn't help smiling. 'You paint quite a picture,' I said. 'You think he's the one who plugged me?'

'I don't know. I can tell you he's not local.'

'Tell me about him?'

'He's your age. Rap sheet as long as your arm. Mostly petty stuff. His driver's license puts him out of San Jose.'

'San Jose!' An invisible spider crawled up my neck.

'That mean something?'

'I'm not sure. Probably not,' I said.

'He told me he was a tourist.'

I look out the window and laughed. It had started to rain, cars hissing by on the wet pavement.

'Last time I looked, this wasn't exactly

a tourist mecca. Was he carrying?'

'Nothing on his person, but I wouldn't be surprised if he had something stashed under the seat. I'd have tossed the car but I had no probable cause and that new rookie was riding along.'

'What, you didn't want to set a bad example?' We shared a quiet laugh.

'I pulled Ratner off to the side for a private chat. Told him if I ran into him again, I'd put a bullet between his eyes and the chief wouldn't blink twice. He turned around and went back the way he came. I don't think he'll be back any time soon.'

We went through another couple beers and smoked up our corner of the room.

'So, what do I do?' I asked, when Frank put on his rain slicker and got ready to leave.

He turned as he walked toward the door. 'I'd suggest you look in your rear-view mirror more often.'

That night my scalp itched fiercely in its healing. I took a few more pills than recommended and dropped down the dark vortex of sleep. I found myself fighting for my life in the sixth round of the Gannon-Antonelli match. At that point we were both about even. He was a tough opponent but I still thought I had a slight edge. Sweat poured off our skins like we were racehorses coming down the home stretch. Blood dripped from a cut above my right eye. I split Vito's upper lip. Blood and sweat sprayed the ringside seats. The crowd rose to its feet with a deafening roar. The betting was heavy, men putting their businesses, their houses, even their marriages on the line.

From the corner of my eye I saw a figure pushing away from the ringside and moving swiftly down the main aisle toward the exit. I glimpsed a waterfall of shiny dark hair, a white suit sprayed with blood, a shimmer of silk stocking.

Laura! Why was she here? What happened to the cab? Where was Jerry?

My moment of distraction was Vito's window of opportunity. The last thing I remember was Jinx barking for me to focus. I never felt the blow that ended my career, my marriage and my dream of climbing the golden ladder to the top.

* * *

I heard Laura calling my name and rolled over in bed. There it was again — the wispy scent of perfume — the silky sound of leaves in the wind. I untangled myself from the sheet and walked to the window, almost expecting her to materialize out of the rain. I leaned against the window frame. Loops of flickering neon from across the street melted into a shifting kaleidoscope of color. A homeless man slept in a cardboard box in the alley beside the pawn shop, a derelict with a bottle in his hand collapsed in the doorway of an old hotel.

Laura, what happened that night? I can't go to my grave not knowing.

I thumbed my Ronson and lit a Lucky. I smoked until my hand stopped shaking, purple ribbons of smoke floating from the tip of my cigarette. The rain came down harder. Suddenly, the scent of perfume drifted away, and I shivered in the draft that rose from the stairwell.

It was then I had an epiphany.

* * *

I met Tully at the door when he arrived the next morning. He yawned and set his car keys on the bar.

'Tell me something,' I said. 'Who told you about Laura dying in that crash?'

'Michael, my eyes aren't open yet.'

'Please, Tully, it's important.'

'Okay, exactly what do you want to know?'

'How did you find out about Laura's death? Was it the radio? The newspaper? What?'

'Give me a minute. It was a long time ago. Okay. I heard it started with a long-distance call from Jerry to Danny Cooney down at the gym. Danny called my brother Tim, and Tim called me.'

'Knowing the information would filter down to me, right?'

'Sure. Within an hour everyone in the Cork knew. Bad news travels fast.' Tully went behind the bar and started setting up. 'Mike, you feeling okay? Have you gone back for your follow-up like you were supposed to?'

'Call Doyle, will ya? I'm going away for a few days.'

* * *

I drove north with my dad's old revolver shoved to the back of the glove compartment. I knew that the answers I was looking for would be in San Jose or nowhere. Mid-afternoon I arrived at the Hall of Records in the Santa Clara County Courthouse. An efficient-looking, grey-haired woman looked at me over her bifocals.

'How may I help you?' she asked.

'I need to locate a death certificate.'

She took a pencil from behind her ear.

'Name of the deceased?'

'Laura Gannon, G-a-n-n-o-n.'

'Your relationship to the deceased?'

'Does it matter?'

'Only if you're requesting a certified copy.'

'Okay, I'll go with that. I was her husband.'

'Date of death?'

'I'm not certain.'

'It's not a trick question, sir.'

'It was a long time ago. I'm not good with dates.'

'How about an educated guess?'

'The thirties. The late thirties.'

'Thank you. I'll be right back.' And she was. Sooner than I expected.

'I'm sorry, sir. I've found nothing under that name. I've checked from thirty-five to forty-two.'

I thought for a moment. 'Try Laura Kelly — with one 'e'. Same timeframe.'

Back again. This time looking slightly bedraggled.

'Sorry, sir. Are you sure you have the right county?'

'One more time. Laura Featherstone.' Once again the clerk returned empty-handed, her glasses slightly askew. She simply shook her head. 'Is this some kind of prank? Are we on *Candid Camera*?'

'Sorry to be such a problem, ma'am. My mother dropped me on my head when I was a baby.'

'I'm so sorry. Would there be a stage name, pen name or *nom de plume*?' she said.

'None comes to mind. Where do I

inquire about marriage licenses?'

She pointed across the aisle and I thanked her for her trouble.

It was there I picked up Laura's paper trail. In ten minutes, for a small fee, I walked out of the building with a copy of the marriage license. In late 1934, Laura Kelly and Jerold G. Featherstone tied the knot in front of a local Justice of the Peace. I was on the right track.

At the phone booth by the curb I looked through the book for Featherstone's number. I'd never known him to give his number to more than a few people, so I wasn't surprised when it wasn't listed. I did, however, find a number for Paul A. Ratner. I was counting on Ratner to lead me to Jerry.

As I exited the booth, a poster tacked to a nearby telephone pole caught my eye. I walked over for a closer look and let out a low whistle. Councilman Jerold G. Featherstone was in a mayoral runoff with City Supervisor, Rufus Kasner. One look at Jerry's smiling photo, with his perfect teeth, golf-course tan and full head of hair, told me he'd aged a hell of a lot better than I had.

I stood mulling things over. Jerry had obviously gone into public service years before and had been climbing the political ladder ever since. Laura's parents died when she was in her teens, so once he'd convinced the people of Santa Paulina that Laura was dead, he didn't have to worry about anyone coming to look for her. In the middle of a campaign, a charge of bigamy against his wife might not go over well with his constituents, and everyone knows how far an opponent will go to dig up dirt. I planned to dig a little dirt myself.

Why Laura hadn't divorced me before she married Jerry is a mystery, but the more I thought about it the better I felt. Our marriage was legal. Jerold G. Featherstone's was not.

* * *

I drove into a rundown section of town not far from Civic Center. Ratner lived in the once-elegant Princess Carlota Hotel. Today it catered to a less affluent clientele than it had eighty years ago. A sign painted on the brick wall of the building advertised rooms for a dollar a day or five dollars by the week. Real classy digs, complete with a community bathroom at the end of the hall and a fire escape that reached five of the twelve stories. A black Buick sedan with a patina of road dust was parked in the back lot.

I bought a hotdog from a street vendor for a dime and ate it behind the hotel as a heavy mist began to sift from the darkening sky. Even a night crawler like Ratner had to slither out from under his rock from time to time. I tossed my napkin into a garbage can and leaned against the building by the back exit.

Sheltering a Lucky from the wind, I had a casual smoke. Within the hour the mist turned to rain. The hotdog vendor pushed his cart beneath the awning of a secondhand store as I listened to water gurgle through the downspout a couple feet away. With Tully and Doyle manning the bar, I had all the time in the world.

Halfway through my third smoke, the back door of the hotel burst open, snapping me to attention. A tall, bony fellow flew through the air and skidded across the concrete on his hands and knees. The door slammed behind him, the deadbolt sliding into place. The suitcase he carried burst open on impact. It looked like everything he owned had been stuffed inside. I flicked my cigarette into the rain.

I pulled Ratner to his feet with one hand and stuck a gun in his ribs with the other. He threw his arms in the air. 'Wait a minute, man! If I had cash, I'd still have my room.'

'So, after that long drive to Santa Paulina, Featherstone stiffed you.'

'Who the hell are you?' His jaw dropped. 'You're him. You're Gannon.'

I frisked him and he was clean.

'Where's your piece?' I said.

'When he didn't pay me, I pawned it.'

I believed him.

'Your clothes are getting wet. Get your stuff. We'll talk in my car.'

'How do I know I can trust you?'

'You can't.'

I pocketed my gun. The poor bastard

had no place to go and no money to get there. I let him put the suitcase in his trunk. It held a jack and a spare — no weapons, no dead bodies.

'What do you want from me?' he asked, when we settled in the front seat of my car. He patted his empty breast pocket. I recognized the gesture and offered him a Lucky. He took it. When I lit it his eyes lingered covetously on my treasured Ronson, just about the only thing I had left from the old fight days. I snapped it shut and put it back in my pocket.

'I'd like information, for starters. Then we'll see where that takes us.'

'Okay.'

'You got any lingering loyalty toward Featherstone?'

'Not anymore. How did you know he was behind this?'

'It's the only thing that makes sense. Tell me how you and Jerry are connected?'

'It's a long story.'

'And I've come a long way to hear it.'

'We were chummy in high school, but I can't say we were really friends. He was a spoiled rich kid, a golden boy with a dark side. He'd hang out with us kids who lived across the tracks just to flaunt his superiority. All but the lucky few were hungry in those days. For a few bucks he had us at his beck and call. He was on a power trip even then.

'After he finished college back east, we hooked up again. *He* actually called *me*. By then I knew what ponies to bet, where the high-stakes card games were, how to get girls to his hotel room for a threesome.

'I was married by then. Even though me and Brigit weren't together long, I never cheated on her. I was never into the kinky stuff like Jerry was, even after Brigit and me split up. Jerry moved south to manage boxers, and returned to San Jose a few years later with a gorgeous woman at his side. His habits haven't changed. He just has a newer car and a bigger house. What I don't get is, why pay for ground chuck when you've got filet mignon waiting for you at home?'

'You mean Laura.' He nodded. I cracked the window to let out the smoke and the smell of Ratner's cheap cologne. 'Why put a hit on me now, after all these years? He's always known where to find me.'

'Jerry fixed the fight back in thirty-four.'

'I know that, but why? I was making him a bundle back then. He was eating high on the hog.'

'It wasn't about the money, although he made plenty betting on Antonelli that night. It was about Laura. You had her. He wanted her. When a man wants a beautiful woman, especially that kind of man, he'll do whatever it takes to get her.'

He confirmed my growing suspicions. Jerry had stabbed me in the back every which way. I told Ratner to continue.

'He told Laura that you wanted her in the front row for that fight. Jerry knew she couldn't stomach the sight of blood. She lost the baby that night, and he stepped right into your shoes. By the time you came out of the coma, they were gone. It wasn't very long before she was introduced to his dark side. By then she was trapped.'

'I don't get that part. The road runs in both directions.'

'She wasn't just afraid of him. Jerry had her convinced you'd never take her back, your family steeped in all that rigid Catholicism. Then, recently, something changed. She became desperate. Your area code came up on Jerry's phone bill and he went ballistic. She knew where all his skeletons were buried and he was running scared. Now she's being guarded night and day by a washed-up wrestler named Stig Overhalter.

'Tonight Jerry's sponsoring a fundraiser at Veteran's Hall. While he's creating an airtight alibi, Stig is going to take Laura into the Santa Cruz Mountains and eliminate Jerry's problem, permanent-like. By the time he puts a bullet in Laura's head she'll welcome it, if you catch my drift.'

'But the statute of limitations ran out on the Gannon-Antonelli bout years ago.'

'That's true, but the accusation would still ruin his political momentum — that, and the fact that he married a woman who was already married to someone else. People are still a little old-fashioned when it comes to things like that.'

'So, how much time we got?' I said.

'For what?'

'To rescue Laura and screw up his plans, what else?'

'I don't know. How much money you got?'

'Three up front. Three after.'

'The event starts at seven.'

'Okay, this is what I want you to do . . . '

* * *

It was dark and raining hard by the time we'd laid out our plan. Ratner walked to his car with the three hundred dollars in his wallet. I stubbed out my fifth cigarette and spent the next ten minutes trying to cough up my lungs.

The Featherstone house was off Blossom Hill Road at the base of the foothills leading into the mountains. I shifted into low gear and started up the long, steep driveway, rain pinging against the windshield, the wipers working overtime. I parked in a grove of redwoods halfway up the hill, hunched deep into the collar of my coat and walked the last hundred yards.

A large Spanish-style house with elaborate wrought-iron grillwork sat at the end of a circular driveway with a tiled fountain at the center. A ratty old Cadillac I took to be Overhalter's was parked in the three-stall garage. Whatever car Featherstone drove was already gone.

Lights burned brightly on the main floor. I carefully tested the front door but it was locked. I eased through the dripping foliage until I had a view through the living-room window.

Laura was tied to a wooden chair, her wrists bound, her pink dress torn open at the bodice, revealing something white and lacy. Her dark hair was cut shoulder-length now and softened by a few strands of silver, but to me she would always be the same pretty girl who danced at the Cork on St. Patrick's Day those many years ago.

I reached through the grillwork and tapped lightly on the pane. She looked my way, but the light in the room turned the glass into a mirror and she couldn't see beyond it. It confused her. She looked frightened. All I could think to do was tap out an SOS. I did it twice and saw a guarded flicker of hope in her eyes.

A man the size of a hippo entered the room. He had a fireplug neck roped in purple veins. Laura trembled as he untied her ropes and pulled her roughly from the chair. As he dragged her from the room I positioned myself to the side of the front door. I had a momentary fear that he might drag her to the bedroom when I heard footsteps in the front entryway. I pulled the pistol out of my pocket.

Overhalter bunted the door open, pushing Laura in front of him, punching a knee into the small of her back, a hand clutching her hair next to the scalp.

'Stig!' I barked, and saw him jolt.

In that brief moment of distraction, Laura bit his hand and jerked free. She fled into the darkness and disappeared behind the fountain. The gun jumped in my hand as Overhalter rushed me. There was a pop, and a bullet sank into the bulky muscle of his upper left arm. He kept coming like an animal unaware of its wound. This time I aimed for center mass. I pulled the trigger and the gun jammed.

Overhalter was twenty years younger than I was. He outweighed me by one hundred and fifty pounds. In desperation, I stomped on the instep of his foot, and he let out a roar. I was suddenly back on Cork Street, fighting the bully on the block, me being the youngest, smallest kid he could find. I'd taken a fighting stance then, like I did now. Overhalter laughed at me just like the bully had. I could have sworn I heard Jinx's voice in my ear. *You can do it, kid!* I somehow found my inner Corky and landed one crushing blow to his jaw. I laid Overhalter out like I had the bully in front of my dad's bar. Jinx's voice had come out of the crowd. *That boyo has potential.*

I left Overhalter where he lay. Laura ran toward me and I met her halfway. I spun her around and around with the rain spiraling about us. Sometimes there are no words for our deepest emotions, only the feeling of coming home after a long journey. We held one another for a long time, the wind whipping our hair, the rain washing away our tears.

* * *

Jerry stood behind the podium at the front of the room in Veterans' Hall. He told the obligatory jokes to warm up the audience. He talked about lowering taxes, improving schools, reforming the prisons, while Laura and I stood in the shadows at the back of the room. I didn't see Ratner in the crowd, but when I saw Ted Butler, the lead investigative reporter from the *Sentinel*, I knew Ratner had made the promised call. The question-and-answer session began, and Butler raised his hand.

'Yes, Mr. Butler,' said Jerry, all smiles. 'What is your question?'

'Our newspaper ran a very flattering article about you in our Sunday edition last month. It was called: 'Councilman Jerry Featherstone, San Jose's Most Eligible Bachelor.' '

'It was a great piece of writing, Ted.'

'So you recall being interviewed for the article?'

'Well, of course. I appreciate all of your kind words.'

I could see Jerry wondering where this line of questioning was headed.

'I believe the article left the reader with the misconception that you are a single man?'

The wattage of his famous smile dimmed to half.

'It was *your* reporting, Ted. You had free rein to frame it as you chose. I understand the article was very well-received.' A tic played at the corner of his eye.

'The truth is, Councilor, that I had been misled. Recently recovered records indicate that you have been married for a long time. Where is Mrs. Featherstone? Is she chained in the attic like Master Rochester's mad wife? During campaigns, wives are usually at their husbands' sides.'

'That is easily explained. No doubt a clerical blunder of some kind.' He shrugged and laughed, but no one was laughing with him anymore. A buzz of curiosity rippled through the room.

'I have a document here that records your 1934 marriage to a Laura Kelly. Are you telling me that the name doesn't ring a bell? I'd like your comment for the record.'

There was a look of panic in his eyes. Maybe this wasn't the best night to orchestrate his wife's disappearance now that people knew she existed.

At that moment, Laura and I stepped into the light. Jerry's jaw dropped and he turned white. He looked at his wristwatch.

'I think that's all the time we have for tonight, ladies and gentlemen. I thank you all for coming. At a future news conference, I assure you that I will answer each and every question to your satisfaction.'

'Just one more before you go.' The voice came from an elderly man in the back row. 'Back in thirty-four, I remember a boxer named, Michael 'The Mick' Gannon. His wife vanished on the night of — '

But Jerry had already bolted from the stage, leaving behind a room of stunned constituents, his political career sinking faster than the *Titanic.*

* * *

I met Ratner in the parking lot of the Carlota Hotel. He was antsy, like he thought I'd stiff him the same as he'd probably stiffed everybody he'd ever met.

'How did it go?' he asked. 'Did Butler show?'

'He did.'

'Then I kept my end of the bargain.'

'You did.' I handed him the final payment in full. 'I suppose you'll be leaving town now.'

'Not with Rufus Kazner as our next mayor. You see, my sister runs a house on the other side of the tracks. I know for a fact where Kazner spends the evenings his wife thinks he's playing poker with the guys.' He wheezed a laugh. 'Luck is definitely turning in my favor.'

Ratner looked over and saw Laura in the car.

'You got her back.'

'I did.' I pulled out my silver Ronson and my pack of cigarettes. I paused a moment and snapped the lighter shut. I handed Ratner the rest of my smokes, and with a twinge that tugged at my heart, put the lighter in his hand.

'A little bonus,' I said. He looked like I'd handed him the Hope Diamond.

'Thanks, man. You sure?'

'I'm sure.'

I didn't know how to have a conversation or drink a cup of coffee without a cigarette, but I'd have to figure it out. When it's my time to go, I don't want to go like Jinx.

'Now what?' asked Ratner.

'Back to Santa Paulina for me. My stitches come out tomorrow.'

'Yeah, sorry about that.'

'Goodbye, Ratner. Have a good life.'

I drove into the storm. After a few miles, Laura was sleeping lightly against my shoulder. A couple hours out of San Jose found me patting my pockets for cigarettes. Pretty soon I was sifting through the butts in the ashtray. I finally emptied the ashes out the window and watched them blow away on the wind.

God, what I wouldn't give for one more cigarette.

Other titles in the
Linford Mystery Library:

COLIN'S GHOST

Norman Firth

In the uncharted jungle of Peru, explorers Colin Davis and Arthur Birnes find the lost city of Kosan, overflowing with gold and gems. Davis intends to share their discovery with the world, but Birnes has more avaricious aims — and he's ready to murder for them . . . Waiting to meet with an informant, undercover policeman Danny King is instead approached by a young woman who claims she is in danger. And as he escorts her home, Danny is jumped by two thugs . . .

WRAITH OF VENGEANCE

Edmund Glasby

Contemplating a scheme to plunder a sinister Venetian island of a rumoured hoard, a tour company advisor finds more there than he bargained for . . . The group gathered for the reading of a will get the shock of their lives . . . A distant oil-drilling platform endures a bizarre siege . . . A man undergoes a hideous transformation . . . The night shift in a morgue takes a deadly turn . . . In an English village on All Hallows Eve, an ancient evil reawakens. Six tales of horror and the macabre by Edmund Glasby.

SILENCE OF THE BONES

Arlette Lees

Rodeo star Coby Dillon vanishes in a storm on the very evening he was to set up house with his girlfriend Brielle Broussard. Where is he — and what has become of his mentor Dyce Dean Jackson? Meanwhile, Deputy Sheriffs Robely Danner and Frack Tilsley — partners in both work and love — are investigating reports of poisonous contaminated moonshine. And Robely's mother Gladys Calhoun is brutally attacked in the night. All these seemingly disparate events are connected by a thread of blood . . .

THE TOKEN

Gerald Verner

Four murders in just over a month, and not the ghost of a clue as to who has committed them — except that in each case a little silver bell was left on the body of the victim. Under pressure from all quarters, Detective-Inspector Shadgold seeks the help of his friend Trevor Lowe, the famous criminologist. But Lowe has nothing to go on, either — until he is approached by terrified film star Gloria Swayne, who reveals that the first victim of the silver bell killer had been her secret fiancé . . .